JANE AUSTEN —
HER GOLDEN YEARS:

A Historical Novel Highlighting Her Family and Faith

by

Muriel Keller Evans

PRESS

To
Joyce Bown,
my forever friend,
of Steventon, Hampshire,
that lovely little village
where Jane Austen's life
and literary career began!

ACKNOWLEDGEMENTS

This book had its beginnings in a cute country cottage in Steventon, Hampshire! I extend my heartfelt thanks to a triumvirate of anonymous Steventon villagers—cherished friends—who participated energetically in reading the manuscript, offering invaluable suggestions, and assisting in distribution. David Selwyn, Editor of *Collected Poems and Verse of the Austen Family* (Carcanet Press), kindly gave permission for the inclusion of James Edward Austen-Leigh's poem. All other quoted works are in the public domain.

Treasured friends in Euless, Texas, Marsha and Robert Hall, pledged their practical assistance, and encouraged the undertaking from start to finish. Diane Bean and Carol Leland, delightful companions from the Raleigh, North Carolina, area offered their enthusiasm and practical help. Longstanding friends in Cyprus, Angela and David Morris, rendered worthwhile recommendations about content and marketing. My daughters, Susan Evans, and Karen Evans Rumbaugh, also read the manuscript and gave valuable assistance and advice.

Last—but not least—the Lord's eternal encouragement has been motivating me all the days of my life, and especially from the beginning to the end of this project. To Him be the glory!

TABLE OF CONTENTS

JANE AUSTEN—
HER GOLDEN YEARS:
A Historical Novel Highlighting Her Family and Faith

Chapter 1

A Novel Novelist

It is a truth universally acknowledged that a single authoress in possession of three published novels—and a fourth at the printer's—must be in want of yet another promising plot, not to mention an excess of charming characters! Jane Austen—handsome, clever, and poor—with a comfortable home and happy disposition, seemed to unite some of the best blessings of existence; and had lived nearly thirty-nine years in the world with very much to distress and vex her. Our heroine, however, had an elegance of mind which enabled her to rise above most of these difficulties. A country clergyman's daughter, Jane was remarkably able to compose without preaching. And this, coupled with a wit honed and sharpened for any verbal or literary joust, was finally bringing her some success as an anonymous writer. Thus our flourishing, but unavowed, novelist found herself in Georgian London in the year 1815. Plots seemed to be in bud, blossom, and bloom all around her—like the delightful garden of her favourite brother, Henry, as she visited him at 23 Hans Place.

This extraordinary sister and brother were only two of eight siblings from a fascinating English family!

The family of Austen, from Kentish roots, had been long settled in Hampshire. Although their names were not to be found in the *Baronetage of England*, the Rev. George Austen and Cassandra Leigh Austen enjoyed a socially respectable life, sandwiched between the country gentry and the unschooled poor of their country village. They had moved to the parsonage at Deane, Hampshire, immediately following their marriage in Bath in 1764. A classical scholar, he had been known as "the Handsome Proctor" of St. John's College, Oxford, and she was the intelligent niece of Theophilus Leigh, the celebrated Master of Balliol College. In 1768 they moved to the refurbished rectory at nearby Steventon, where the family settled to care for their parish and their young. By 1773 he had been granted the living of Steventon and Deane, becoming Rector of both parishes. Their rural rectory was of modest size for the nurturing of the eight children born to them. But for the past generation they had lived in so respectable a manner as to engage the general good opinion of their surrounding acquaintances. Amazingly, for the era in which they lived, the Austen children all survived to adulthood and were encouraged to find the place in life most suited to their diverse temperaments and giftings.

Henry, our novelist's favourite brother and four years her senior, was a man-about-town in London—a charming, but currently ailing, host to his talented sister. He was an easy-going extrovert who might have followed a career in the Church. Instead, with England at war with Napoleon, he chose to become an Oxfordshire Militiaman. Ever inventive, he used that as a springboard to becoming a fairly wealthy banking partner, with establishments in London and Alton, Hampshire. But an economic downturn following Napoleon's defeat at Waterloo earlier that year was creating the threat of serious failure. He had also, in the past year, lost the love of his life—his socially sophisticated and cosmopolitan cousin, Eliza de Feuillide. Henry put on a cheerful face, but Jane sensed the stress and struggle within that may have weakened his usually robust constitution. Henry had always kept a brotherly eye on Jane and had been most helpful in the difficult task of negotiating with his sister's publishers. He was exceedingly proud of her literary prowess—so proud that during the famed Dr. Baillie's previous visit, Henry had disclosed that she was the anonymous authoress of the latest rage in novels—*Sense and Sensibility, Pride and Prejudice*, and *Mansfield Park*. The doctor had informed Jane that the Prince Regent admired her work greatly and had copies of each in every one of his palaces.

"Henry, how could you?" scolded Jane gently, as she tenderly nursed her very ill brother. For the umpteenth time that day she removed the damp cloth on his forehead and replaced it with a cooler one, for his fever had intensified and would dry them out almost as soon as she applied them. Madame Bigeon, his faithful housekeeper, flitted in and out of the sickroom, muttering mournfully in French as she kept the sickroom supplied with all that was necessary.

"I couldn't help myself," replied Henry, weakly, for the bilious fever that had reduced him to being a helpless invalid had taken its toll on his voice as well as his body. Jane smiled wryly at him, trying to put on a cheerful face. But the truth was she was very concerned about this dearest of brothers, for she had never known him to be so gravely ill. He had fought bravely the past few days, but now seemed to be losing the battle. Jane just couldn't bear to lose Henry! They had asked his regular doctor, the young Charles Haden, to attend him at first, but as the fever progressed and the pain increased, Dr. Haden recommended the royal family's doctor, Matthew Baillie. Jane consoled herself momentarily that this most noted of doctors in London would return to visit him soon—that same Dr. Baillie, who attended the Prince Regent and to whom Henry had recently revealed her authorship.

As she pondered the gravity of the situation, there was a knock at the outer door, and soon Madame Bigeon showed the celebrated doctor into the room. The Scotsman greeted Jane curtly with a nod of the head as he scrutinised the patient carefully. Laying his hand on Henry's forehead and then carefully checking his pulse, the doctor shot a quick glance at Jane which communicated his mounting concern over Henry's deteriorating condition. Henry moaned softly as he tried to shift his position in the bed, but had not the strength to do so. Jane watched as Dr.Baillie opened his bag and took out a vial of laudanum, from which he poured a few drops into a glass of water. He administered it to the patient, who swallowed with difficulty, and then lay heaving on the bed from the exertion. The celebrated doctor motioned Jane to follow him outside the door of the room.

"Miss Austen, I'm sorry to be the bearer of bad news, but your brother's situation is growing alarmingly serious. I'm sure his fever and erratic breathing have not escaped your notice. I cannot disguise the fact that I am extremely concerned about him. In fact, I fear that in his weakened state he may not be with us for much longer."

Jane's eyes grew wide with alarm, and her breath came in short gasps, as she cried, "But, doctor...he's so young... for this to happen...he has always been so full of life and energy....I...I understand you're doing...everything in your power...to bring the fever under control...and to make him well again....What...what do you think is best to be done?"

"I would urge you to dispatch an express letter to your family members and let them know that his state of health is very precarious. I'm afraid if they want to see him alive, they must make haste to come to London as soon as they can make the journey. I'm afraid I have done all I can."

Jane was stunned, not only by his words, but by his grave demeanour. In the time he had been attending Henry, she had never seem him quite so serious. "Yes...of course, doctor... I'll do as you say...immediately." She stood staring in blank amazement as he nodded and took his leave. Jane shook her head and tried to rally her senses to the importance of the task at hand. She had never sent an express in her life before and had absolutely no idea as to how to go about it. The weight of it all settled upon her in that moment, and she felt as if she might crumple to the floor. Steadying herself against the wall, she slowly raised her gaze upward, and with an agonising sob, cried out, "Dear God...please...help...me!"

A sharp knock at the outer door startled her, and she turned to see Madame Bigeon's daughter scurrying to open it. In the dim light of the hallway, she could make out the form of Dr. Charles Haden, Henry's former doctor, coming toward her. "Miss Austen," I saw Dr. Baillie getting into his carriage on my way in. I hope Henry is not worse since I was here last? But I see from the anxiety on your face that all is not well. What...what can I do to be of service?"

"Oh," she cried, "you've come at just the right moment! The doctor is so concerned about Henry that he has advised me to send an express to the family, advising them of his... precarious situation. But here in London I have no idea of knowing how to do it...and I don't seem to have the strength." As the words tumbled out of Jane, she struggled to keep control of her voice and sounded dangerously close to tears. Dr. Haden, observing her consternation and only too glad to find something practical to do, immediately proposed that she get the addresses and let him take care of the expresses.

"Oh, would you?" replied Jane, and moved quickly in the direction of the study to write the necessary information. She was back within minutes, and handed the paper to him. Looking anxiously into his face, she choked out, "Please, oh please, hurry. I could never forgive myself if Henry...died...

without the members of his family around him! We've... always been so close," she finished lamely, sitting down awkwardly on the nearest chair. "I'm sorry, I just feel so weak at the moment; I can't stand up any longer."

He looked closely at her with concern in his face. "Please, don't apologise, Miss Austen. I know how much you love Henry and how important his family is to him. I'll dispatch the expresses immediately. Is there anything else I can do to help?"

"No, no, that is what is of utmost need at the moment. I can send for Dr. Baillie if he gets worse,. But I had better get back to Henry, for I fear he needs my constant attention. Thank you," she said, rising unsteadily from the chair and heading slowly back to Henry's sickroom. After Madame Bigeon showed him out, she urged Jane to let her or her daughter keep vigil in the sickroom. But this faithful servant throughout the years Eliza was living, was even more distraught than Jane and sorely in need of rest. Reluctantly she submitted to Jane's entreaties otherwise, imploring her to not hesitate to disturb her if Henry's condition should change for the worse.

Jane sat close to Henry throughout the night, holding his hand and praying fervently for his life to be spared. The laudanum seemed to have taken effect and he was resting more comfortably now. She leaned closer to hear his halting breathing, hoping with all her heart that her family members could come speedily. She had never felt so alone in her life! Frank and Charles, the two youngest brothers closest to her in age, were Navy men at sea and not in a situation to receive a letter for weeks. An express had been sent to James, her eldest brother, now Rector of St. Nicholas Church in Steventon. He would undoubtedly go to Chawton and collect their only sister, Cassandra, and bring her with him. She knew Martha Lloyd, the sisters' friend from their youth, would willingly care for their elderly mother while Cassandra was away from the home their brother, Edward, had provided for them in Chawton. He was a year older than Henry and had been adopted in his teen years by a rich cousin. She knew Edward had the means to come quickly from Kent in his chaise-and-four and would likely be the first of her siblings to arrive in London. But travel was slow and difficult, and she knew it might be days, rather than hours!

Between her ministrations to Henry, she dozed fitfully by his bedside, as her thoughts rambled in and out of consciousness—a jumble of reality and the surreal. How could she ever carry on without Henry? Would she ever, at this late stage of her life, find anyone of his inestimable worth? Maybe her early attraction to Tom Lefroy had been because he was witty and charming like Henry. Perhaps, too, that was the reason she had turned down Harris Bigg-Wither's proposal—or rather broken her overnight engagement to him—because he did not measure up to this best of brothers. She thought of Henry's winsome personality and all his fine capabilities—so different from George, their second brother. He was born with a mental handicap and was being cared for, along with his similarly afflicted maternal uncle, by a couple in a Hampshire village. His brothers had contributed to his upkeep and made a point of visiting him fairly frequently. They always reported him in good health physically, but it was some time since she had seen him, and she wondered how he was faring.

Her thoughts continued to meander to characters in her novels who had been at the bedside of a gravely ill loved one—Elinor, when her sister, Marianne, was near death's door, in *Sense and Sensibility*, and Edmund, at his brother Tom's bedside, in *Mansfield Park*, when he was so severely ill. Astonishing that what had been a figment of her own imagination had now become such a real part of her own life! As the long night wore on, her mind wandered to her precious father, who had died of a similar fever almost ten long years ago. He had lingered only two days with it, and then unbelievably, was gone! Jane's heart ached for his gentle presence, and she longed to have his comfort now. A moan from Henry startled her out of her reverie, and she awoke to see daylight creeping around the edges of the heavy draperies.

The day moved painfully slowly, as Madame Bigeon gave Jane some respite and tried to get her to take a little nourishment. "Ma petite, you must eat to keep up your strength," she implored. Jane did her best to choke down some soup at midday, but she had no appetite for it. During the late afternoon Henry rallied sufficiently to request that she read the 23rd Psalm to him, and she watched as his parched lips did their best to form the familiar words:

> *The Lord is my shepherd; I shall not want.*
> *He maketh me to lie down in green pastures:*
>   *he leadeth me beside the still waters.*
> *He restoreth my soul: he leadeth me in the*
>   *paths of righteousness for his name's sake.*
> *Yea, though I walk through the valley of*
>   *the shadow of death, I will fear no evil:*
>   *for thou art with me; thy rod and*
>   *thy staff they comfort me.*
> *Thou preparest a table before me in the*
>   *presence of mine enemies: thou anointest*
>   *my head with oil; my cup runneth over.*
> *Surely goodness and mercy shall follow me*
>   *all the days of my life: and I will dwell in*
>   *the house of the Lord for ever.*

It seemed to bring him some comfort, and he smiled wanly when she had finished. She thought she saw a glint in his inflamed eyes, but couldn't tell whether it was joy or tears, and she had to turn away hastily before she choked up herself. It was a long time since she had felt such emotional turmoil, and she steeled herself forcibly, trying to get her emotions under control. When would James and Cassandra arrive to help bear the crushing burden she felt? Was Edward even at home in Kent to receive the express, or was he on a journey of which she was unaware? She couldn't expect any of them today, could she? There would be yet another agonising night of being alone with her fears and the exhaustion that was slowly overtaking her senses. Oh, how could she ever handle it?

It was then that the noise of a carriage intruded upon her jumbled thoughts. She hurried to the window and stared out into the blackness, discerning in the dim lamplight that it was indeed Edward's livery. She opened the front door as quickly as she could, for Madame Bigeon had been persuaded to take some rest as night fell, and Jane was loathe to disturb her. Edward came bounding up the steps, exclaiming, "Jane, Jane, I came as quickly as I could. Am in in time. Is he...?" But Edward couldn't complete his sentence, for his sister slumped heavily against him and the tears poured forth, as sobs shook her whole body. In an instant he realised the incredible strain she had been under and did his best to lead her to the sofa in the Sitting Room. Edward wasn't good at dealing with emotions, but he tried to calm her: "It's all right now. I'm here. I will see to everything. Do not worry, Jane." She raised a tear-stained face to his, but all she could do was shake her head in weak affirmation, for no sound would come. "I'll stay with Henry tonight. You go to your room and try to sleep, for you look completely exhausted," he urged. After a long moment, she rose unsteadily and led the way to Henry's room, managing to give him some whispered instructions regarding the patient's care. Then, with a wistful look at Henry and Edward, she wended her way wearily to her bed and sank, fully clothed, into an exhausted sleep.

The next morning she awoke with a start. Dawn had broken, and daylight was streaming through the open curtains. For a moment, nothing would come into focus. But then the reality of Henry's precarious situation penetrated her senses, and she remembered that Edward had arrived. She rose quickly, realising she hadn't even undressed the night before, and made a hasty *toilette*. Moving in the direction of the sickroom, she passed Madame Bigeon in the hallway, carrying more cool cloths to the patient. As she looked intently into the darkened room, Edward rose from his chair and came toward her.

"How is he?" was her first response.

"He had a restless night, but seems quieter now. I'm not a good judge of these things, Jane, but it appears to me his breathing is not as laboured as it was when I first saw him. Come and see for yourself," he said, taking her by the arm and gently steering her in the direction of the chair by the bed. As she watched the steady rise and fall of Henry's chest, the first glimmer of hope began to stir in her heart. She felt Henry's head, which still seemed very hot to her touch, and with that he stirred and opened his eyes. They were glazed, but comprehending, as he took in the fact that Edward was standing there with his sister. He tried to speak, but all he could manage was a hoarse whisper, "What...?"

"Shhhh," both of them remonstrated at the same instant. An amused look crept over their faces as they glanced quickly at one another. There was a hint of a smile on Edward's lips as he turned back to the patient and continued talking to him in hushed tones. Jane crept to the foot of the bed and gazed at them both with admiration in her eyes. She had to admit she wasn't as close to Edward, or any of her other brothers for that matter, as she was to Henry—except, perhaps, for her particular little brother, Charles, now away at sea.

Edward had been adopted in his teens by the Knights— childless, rich cousins of their father's, who lived in Kent.

She had visited him there at Godmersham as often as she could. But even if this brother wasn't as high as Henry in her esteem—and Jane felt sometimes that Edward was a little spoiled—she had to acknowledge he was the practical one in the family, a little like Frank, and certainly took responsibility seriously. In fact, he was probably more responsible than Henry! As a widower, Edward was no stranger to tragedy, for his beloved Elisabeth had died birthing their eleventh child, and Jane knew he grieved for her even now... and probably always would. She sensed that his grief had softened the abrasiveness she had sometimes experienced in her relationship with him, and she suddenly saw him in a new light at her brother's bedside! How grateful she was for his strength, and thankful from the bottom of her heart that he had responded so quickly. Now if Cassandra and James would just come, she knew she would feel much better.

It was to be another full day before they would arrive, during which Dr. Baillie came and went, saying little, but still looking very grave. Finally Jane heard the welcome sounds of James' carriage drawing up in front of the house. As they alighted and came into the hall, she clung to her elder sister, unwilling and unable to let go of her for several wordless minutes. Used to such display of emotion between the sisters, James hastily pecked Jane on the cheek and headed immediately to the sickroom to join his brothers. He had expected that Edward would have arrived before him, for Edward had the resources to travel more swiftly. Cassandra intuitively sensed everything Jane could not express and just patted her gently until she looked up with grateful tears in her eyes. "Oh, Cassandra," was all she could say over and over, as her sister continued to make soothing sounds that gradually brought her around.

Jane managed to release her just long enough to let her take off her pelisse. Madame Bigeon, by then, was fussing around them, murmuring in French all the while, and making herself useful by bringing refreshment for the weary travellers. They moved quietly into Henry's room, trying not to disturb the patient. Cassandra took Henry's hand in hers and patted it tenderly, as she smiled reassuringly into his wondering eyes. She sensed that he could not quite understand what all the fuss was about, but seemed grateful to have his siblings around him. Cassandra and Jane sat up with their brother that night, allowing their brothers to sleep. They sat, content in each other's company, praying together and sharing feelings too deep for words, asking that their brother's life might be spared.

Day dawned with a cold drizzle running slowly down the windowpanes. Jane rose and stretched, feeling somewhat cheered, now that her long, lonely vigil was over. She had gained inward strength from the night spent in her sister's warm emotional embrace, and for the first time she felt she could face whatever the day might bring forth. Heaven seemed to have heard their impassioned appeal, for Henry's fever appeared to have abated somewhat, and the patient was stirring restlessly, attempting to move in his bed. Cassandra plumped his pillows and helped him to some water, receiving a glimmer of a smile for her efforts. Jane stood by her side, trying to assess her brother's situation objectively. Did Henry appear improved because she herself was feeling better? Was he past the worst or heading for a relapse? She realized she could only be subjective about someone so close to her, and decided to leave it to the doctor to make the pronouncements. He was calling on his daily rounds while Henry's health was at such a critical stage. The brothers joined them and thought there might be some improvement, but decided to leave it to the medical man.

Madame Bigeon had prepared a bountiful breakfast for them all and persuaded them to leave Henry in her care while they refreshed themselves. The conversation was animated in a muted sort of way, for they all felt their brother's situation too keenly to be in high spirits. But it felt good to be together again, talking of family matters in familiar ways and sharing experiences that bound them as siblings. They talked soberly of the difficulties Henry was facing in the banking industry, as the economy floundered following the end of the Napoleonic wars. They all were aware, but nobody mentioned, that Edward and their mother's brother, Uncle Leigh-Perrot, had large sums invested in his banks. During the far-ranging discussion, Edward intimated that he also was facing difficulties, as an inheritance claim had been instituted by several people against his estate in Chawton. He might not have much choice other than to cut down a swath of mature trees on the estate to raise sufficient funds to satisfy their demands.

Doing her best to move the conversation to more uplifting topics, Jane enquired of James as to the wellbeing of his Anna, James Edward, and Caroline. All three had shown a propensity for writing, under their father's careful guidance, for he had a literary gift of a poetic nature. She was reminded that James and Henry, as well as their father, had helped to shape her own literary career when she was a young girl, guiding her choice of literature. Jane promised to write to these nieces and nephews, encouraging them in their literary endeavours. Edward was plied with questions about his brood, especially Fanny, who was almost like another sister to Jane. And she discovered that his William, who had long been a favourite with her, was considering following in his grandfather's footsteps, moving steadily toward taking Holy Orders and being the future rector of St. Nicholas Church, Steventon. Edward was even considering building him a new rectory on higher ground, for the basements in the one where they had been raised were constantly damp, particularly in the Spring season.

While they were still at breakfast, Dr. Baillie arrived, and they could tell by the relieved look on his face that the patient was past the danger point. "I'm going to err on the side of caution," he said, "but I believe we have seen a marked improvement in your brother. If he carries on steadily in this course, I think there is room for optimism about his making a slow, but full, recovery." The relief was evident in their faces, as the men shook hands with him, and the ladies nodded their grateful appreciation. James exclaimed, "The Lord be praised!" and hurried to Henry's room as soon as the doctor departed. The others followed, and rarely was there a sickroom more full of emotion—expressed and unexpressed—as there was that day at 23 Hans Place in London! Edward departed on the morrow, for he had pressing business on his three estates. James and Cassandra lingered longer, but James was anxious to be off, as he must make preparations for Divine Service on Sunday at Steventon and Deane. It was a relieved Jane who finally bid them adieu— with reluctance, but sincere gratitude—promising to write her sister at the earliest possible moment!

Chapter 2

A Letter to Cassandra

23 Hans Place, London

My dearest Cassandra,

I trust that your journey home with James was without incident and that you were able to rest after such an anxious trip and the terrible ordeal through which we have all passed. How I miss you already, and you have been gone but a day! Only you will know how relieved I felt when you arrived here last week. The long and harrowing days leading up to your visit were almost more than I could bear! I know how difficult it was for you to leave your responsibilities with our mother in Chawton, but I will be forever grateful that you made such haste in coming. What would I have ever done without you? Please do express my thanks to our dear friend, Martha Lloyd, for bearing the brunt of our mother's inquietude during your absence. But I know you are anxious for news of our Henry!

Dr. Baillie has been to see him again this morning—probably for the last time—and finds him remarkably improved. Indeed, the patient is being encouraged to sit up in a chair as much as possible and to walk about a little. He leans on me heavily, of course, but it is good to see him showing such improvement. His spirits are much cheered, and his sense of humour has much more play than you saw before your departure. I confess I spend a good deal of time just looking at him and contemplating how close he came to leaving us. Indeed, the doctor had given up all hope of his recovery, or I would not have alarmed you with an express. We well know that it is because of the Lord's goodness and mercy that he was not taken from us.

Looking back on those dark days, I cannot help but feel that you and I were like Martha and Mary beseeching the Lord to intervene lest our Lazarus die! Praying together with you brought strength that I do not feel when I am on my own. Truly, two are better than one. You alone, dear sister, know how devastating it would have been for me to lose Henry—almost as great as losing you would be! I am just realising afresh that he and I have a closeness that is very rare between brother and sister. Since his dear Eliza departed this world, it seems he and I delight even more in each other's company. And, as you well know, Henry's help in getting my manuscripts published has been vital to me. I could not face being on my own to deal with London publishers!

Henry's closeness to death has made me consider the deaths we have already experienced of loved ones dear to our family. When I look back, I realize how often we have had to say goodbye to those who were so near to us. There are so many! Even before our esteemed father's death, there was James' Anne—and after only three years of marriage. Will we ever forget their precious little Anna toddling around our house calling out forlornly for her mama? And then Edward's beloved Elisabeth, perishing so soon after the birth of their eleventh child. How brave of their Fanny at 16 to step in and take her place as hostess as best she could? It is just over a year since our particular little brother, Charles, lost his Fanny during the birth of their fourth child on board his ship. How difficult is childbearing for those of our sex! It is something I have never had the desire to endure. And then, Henry had to give up his Eliza after her long struggle. That leaves only our brother, Frank, with his Mary, and heaven only knows what may be in store for them. I admit this had made me ponder anew the brevity of this life and to place my hope afresh in our Saviour—that in the life to come we will be united with them all and that there will be no more sorrow or tears!

Enough of such serious discussion; let me turn to what will make you smile. I have another of my own dear children in hand—just delivered from the publisher. I am beginning to correct the proofs of *Emma*, which came shortly after you departed. I find it a rather pleasant distraction to bury myself in that little country village of Highbury for an hour or two while the patient is resting. Indeed, Henry has begged that I read it aloud to him. Dear Dr. Perry, of that tiny village, seems to have grown in my estimation since I last wrote about him!

It is astonishing to think that this is now the fourth novel that has come from my pen. The ideas continue to bubble forth like an artesian well. I will be sitting, thinking about nothing in particular, and suddenly a phrase or a sentence will spring to mind. I have to run and jot it down before it completely disappears. It is as if I'm being borne along on a current that ebbs and flows and sometimes eddies in small circles. It is truly exhilarating!

I was just remembering an incident which occurred long ago when you were about fifteen and I was twelve. We were sitting in Steventon Church on a rainy, drizzly day, when our father was speaking on the text, "We have gifts differing, according to the grace given us." I believe I remember it so well because papa was saying that our gifts operate by faith—as simple as that of a child—and he had requested that you teach the children a song from the Sunday School children's movement. The words were (do you still remember?):

> *Jesus wants me for a sunbeam,*
> *To shine for Him each day;*
> *In every way try to please Him*
> *At home, at school, at play.*

> *A sunbeam, a sunbeam,*
> *Jesus wants me for a sunbeam;*
> *A sunbeam, a sunbeam,*
> *I'll be a sunbeam for Him!*

I remember that my heart was stirred that day—not just by the words of the song—but by the fact that as you were leading us in singing, the sun broke forth and beamed through the narrow window directly on you. That is one of the indelible pictures that I carry around in my mind. As I looked at you, bathed in that sunlight, I wanted to be just like you. I prayed fervently that the Lord would help me to have the faith of a little child (papa always talked about that), so that I could be a sunbeam for Him. I can recall being very much moved by papa's sermon that day on using our gifts to further God's kingdom. I didn't know for sure what my gifts were, but I hoped that one of them might be writing. I don't remember that I ever shared that with you, but it is something I will always carry with me in my mind and in my heart.

Enough of reminiscing! I do hope that my writing *is* having a moral effect on the inhabitants of England. I think I must write something soon that will enhance the reputation of those brave men, like our brothers Frank and Charles, who are serving in His Majesty's Navy. I think I can work a little romance into that if I try very hard!

I would write more, but I want to be careful of your purse. Take care, dear sister.

Always affectionately yours,
Jane

Chapter 3

A Court Visitor

Jane was more light of foot than she had been for a long time, as she tripped around Henry's London residence, cheerfully taking care of all his needs. She could tell he was improving every day, as his list of wants became ever longer! Now he was able to be out in the garden on sunny days, relaxing on the *chaise longue* that had been placed there for him. Jane sat in a chair by his side, working carefully on correcting the proofs of *Emma* for Mr. John Murray, her current publisher. If this fourth novel would just sell as well as had her other three, she would no longer have such a dreadful propensity for being poor!

"I am not sure many people will like this latest heroine of mine, Henry," she exclaimed as she glanced up momentarily from her proofreading.

"How could anyone not like one of your heroines, Jane?" he commented, looking up fondly at his devoted nurse. "Although I think you might have a difficult time improving on Fanny," he added.

"Well, I admit that this one is certainly a far cry from the one in *Mansfield Park,* but we shall just have to see whether others like her as much as I do."

They were interrupted at that moment by Madame Bigeon, who bustled out into the garden to announce a rather distinguished visitor for Jane. She handed his calling card to the astonished lady.

"Why, Henry, it is James Stanier Clarke, the Prince Regent's Chaplain and Royal Librarian. I cannot imagine what he would want with me."

"Can you not?" replied Henry, his eyes twinkling and a smile twitching at the corners of his mouth.

"I am certainly not going to meet with him on my own," she murmured, half to herself. "Bid him come and join us in the garden," she said hesitantly, and then stared intently at Madame Bigeon's figure disappearing into the house. Life was definitely not dull at Henry's house in London!

The Rev. Clarke soon presented himself, proffering a deep bow to Jane and Henry and seating himself with a grand flourish in the cushioned chair that was offered him. Jane noted that he was not very tall, quite plump, had a rather pleasant countenance, and appeared to be around fifty years of age. "My dear Madam," he began with polished ease, "I am commanded by His Royal Highness, the Prince Regent, to wait upon you this very afternoon. I have been instructed to pay you every possible attention and to invite you to visit Carlton House to see the Library and the other fine apartments there." He paused in his oration to take in his listener's reaction.

But where he was expecting enthusiasm and excitement, he was met with only bewilderment and confusion. "My dear Sir," exclaimed Jane, her cheeks reddening, why would His Royal Highness be interested in inviting me to tour his palace?

"Why, you cannot imagine, Miss Austen, how thrilled the Prince Regent was to discover from Dr. Baillie the name of the authoress of his three favourite novels—and to learn that she was currently in London! Why, he is a great admirer of yours, and has bound copies of each set in every one of his residences. I can attest that he reads them regularly, too."

Jane glanced at her beaming brother and murmured, "Look what a Pandora's Box you have opened for me now, Henry."

"My dear Miss Austen, are you not pleased that your work has been brought to the attention of the future King of this glorious realm?" inquired Rev. Clarke, incredulity in his voice.

"Why, I suppose I am," was her mild response. But seeing that the Prince Regent's messenger was looking sadly deflated at her lack of enthusiasm, she made an effort to brighten up and added, "And, Sir, I will be pleased to accept the kind invitation of His Royal Highness to Carlton House."

At that point they agreed on a date for the visit a fortnight hence in the afternoon, determining that Jane would be accompanied by Madame Bigeon, as Henry was not yet well enough to walk at any length. As they chatted, that fine lady appeared and served tea for them all in the garden. As they enjoyed the delicious repast, Rev. Clarke relaxed a little and began to expand on his honours and distinctions at Court, sounding a little too much to Jane and Henry like Mr. Collins in *Pride and Prejudice*. "You cannot imagine how gracious is my Lord and Master in condescending to grant me the exalted titles of Chaplain of the Royal Household and Librarian. I assure you that in this latter capacity I have worked diligently to transform the Prince's extensive library, bringing it into a state of orderliness, cataloguing and binding the books, and initiating a very useful index. Indeed, I have brought order out of chaos—which is a Godlike quality, do you not agree?"

Jane, like Lizzy in *Pride and Prejudice*, did her best to stifle her amusement at this ridiculous display of pomposity, good-humouredly congratulating him on his achievements.

Henry sought to turn the conversation into another vein by introducing the subject of the Royal Navy and the struggle of their two worthy brothers, Charles and Francis, to climb the ladder of the Admiralty ranks. Again, the Rev. Clarke plunged into a robust personal history of his previous career as Chaplain on His Majesty's Ships, *Jupiter* and *Impeteux*. "Imagine the energy and exertion required of me to perform Divine Service on deck twice a day, as well as a Sunday sermon and commital services for all those unfortunates whose bodies had to be consigned to the deep. I assure you it was not a task for the fainthearted," he concluded grandly.

But then went rushing on, "And, of course, I had the inestimable honour of being of the party that conducted Her Serene Highness, Princess Caroline of Brunswick from Germany to England for her marriage to the Prince Regent. "Yes," he mused, "I was called upon to say grace at the sumptuous dinner for her onboard the *Jupiter*, and to perform Divine Service that Sunday afternoon. I must confess she has always received me cordially and with great condescension during the times I saw her at the palace, especially shortly after the birth of the Princess Charlotte. That baby has grown into quite a romantic young lady, and" he lowered his voice significantly, "should soon be married, as you may have heard. But, of course, her mother is no longer part of the royal household."

"It is fascinating that our brother, Francis, was on board the *Lark* that was part of the expedition to escort Princess Caroline to England for the royal nuptials. Did you happen to meet him, Mr. Clarke?, questioned Henry, breaking into his monologue.

"Well, well, so that was your brother!" he replied. "The crewmen certainly gave the *Lark* a rousing welcome when they hove into view after being lost five days in the fog," he laughed. "But, of course, your brother was not captain of that ship when they went off on their lark," he winked, proud of his obvious pun.

The conversation might have gone on in that vein interminably, except that at this moment Rev. Clarke noticed the manuscript Jane had been correcting and had put to one side. "Another novel being readied for printing, Miss Austen?" he inquired.

"Why, yes," she replied, "I am just putting the final touches to it."

"Splendid!" exclaimed the visitor. "The Prince Regent required me to ascertain whether you had any more novels in hand, and instructed me to give you leave to dedicate the next one to him," he stated triumphantly.

Jane looked quickly at her brother out of the corner of her eye, knowing exactly what he was thinking, for he knew how much she detested the morals of the dissolute future George IV. She hesitated for a moment, mentally weighing the implications of such a situation. Should she outright refuse the wishes of the reigning Regent of the realm? Realising in an instant the consequences of such a course of action, she raised her gaze to meet that of Rev. Clarke and replied, somewhat tersely, "The Prince Regent's wish is my command."

"Good. Now that it's all settled, I shall take my leave. It has been a great pleasure meeting both of you. I shall take the liberty of informing His Royal Highness that you will be visiting Carlton House in the near future and that you will be dedicating your next novel to him. It is a privilege and an honour to be the bearer of such welcome news." Jane rose to see the visitor out, but he demurred, remarking that the servant could conduct him through the house to his waiting carriage.

After he left the garden, Jane sat silently staring into the distance, pondering the events of the last hour. Henry knew her reflective moods and didn't attempt to interrupt her thoughts until she finally stirred from her reverie. "Well,

Jane, with *Emma* dedicated to the Prince Regent, that should sell a few extra copies, eh?" he suggested. "It will help swell your bank account, little sister," he continued, more seriously. He knew this was a touchy point with Jane, for she longed to be financially independent. Even her sister had the interest from the one thousand pounds her *fiance*, Tom Fowle, had left her when he died unexpectedly of Yellow Fever in the West Indies. She, alone, of all the Austen siblings, except poor George, had had no personal income until her first novel came off the press four years earlier. And even with three novels in circulation, she still had not accumulated the amount her sister had safely invested. It was a difficult life for a spinster in the nineteenth century!

Jane shook her head in disbelief, "I am still so utterly amazed at this turn of events that I can't even contemplate the consequences. I suppose John Murray will be pleased, but I cannot help but feel that any association with such a contemptible rake as the Prince Regent can bring me no credit. He has so many mistresses, one cannot keep track of them. And he has treated his wife, Princess Caroline, so abominably, I cannot ever think well of him!" Such vehemence Henry knew not to counter, although he agreed with her thoroughly. Instead he suggested they move inside, as a late afternoon chill had begun to set in

A few days later, when Henry had regained more of his strength, he surprised Jane by suggesting that they go for a ride in his curricle. It had been over a month since he had been out in it, and as the day was quite mild, he thought it would be a pleasant diversion. But he had another purpose in mind.

"What would you say, Jane, to our stopping in Bond Street to do a bit of shopping?" he queried.

"Do you have anything particular in view?" she asked, searching his face for unspoken clues.

"Why, I thought you might enjoy showing up at Carlton House in a dress of the latest fashion," he chuckled, with a twinkle in his eye.

"Henry!" she exclaimed, "I have been pondering what to wear, for as you know, I have nothing very grand in my wardrobe."

"Then let this be your reward for nursing me through my illness and convalescence. I owe you a great debt, Jane" he finished tenderly, looking seriously into her eyes.

"Nonsense, Henry," she replied. "You have been helping me at every turn since I was a child, and there is nothing I could do for you to repay that debt.

So, with that settled, they rode cheerfully together through the crowded streets of London in his curricle. When they reached Bond Street, Henry halted the fashionable vehicle at one of Eliza's favourite *couturiers*, and ushered Jane into the shop. Henry sat, while Jane sorted carefully through the materials and designs that were available. Eventually she selected a rich plum-coloured silk of exceptional quality, which was on at a very good sale price. The French-*emigree* proprietor, whom Henry knew personally, assured her the gown would be ready within the week, and promised to bring it to Hans Place for a fitting in the next few days. Jane left the shop with a sample of the material, humming happily along the way as Henry and she drove home. It had been a long time since she had felt such sheer exhilaration!

The day of the fitting came and went, and Jane was pleased with the result. However, as the date for her visit to Carlton House approached, she began to experience a measure of disquietude. After all, she had never been to a Prince's palace before, and she was not looking forward wholeheartedly to the encounter with Rev. Clarke on her own. How she wished Henry could go with her! But she noticed the exertion of his drive in the curricle to Bond Street had set him back a little, and she was not willing to risk his health on behalf of her comfort.

Henry noticed her inner restlessness as the event drew closer and tried to allay her concerns: "It's a great honour to receive such an invitation, Jane, and Carlton House is reputed to be sumptuous," he began.

She interrupted him before he could go any further with the brotherly lecture on which he was embarking, "It's not difficult for you, Henry, to move about with ease in society, for your personality is very outgoing, and you are comfortable even with strangers. But, as you well know, I struggle in that area and tend to be less sure of myself in social situations."

"Yes, I have to admit I am energized by being in company—and particularly fine company. One of the times I most enjoyed was being invited to the grand gala at Burlington House last year, where the Czar of Russia, the King of Prussia, and the Prince of Austria were feted. Do you remember my telling you?"

"Of course I do, Henry, but that's hardly relevant to my situation," she stated a little petulantly.

"Now, Jane, you have met Rev. Clarke, and he seems an affable enough fellow, even if he is a little pompous. You have great fortitude and always rise to the occasion, dear sister. Do you recall the evening you met the celebrated French hostess, Madame de Stael, here at one of Eliza's little *soirees*? You carried yourself admirably through that evening, Jane. And I have high hopes that you will enjoy this little escapade and be able to gather inside information for one of your future novels," he countered.

This brought a slight smile to Jane's tight lips. Henry knew how to handle her in a way her other brothers did not, and she was grateful for such intuition and understanding on his part. "Oh, what a Henry!" she remarked, as she turned on her heel and left him chuckling.

The trepidation had not dissipated by the next afternoon, when Jane was dressed and looking particularly charming in her new plum-coloured silk. Madame Bigeon's daughter had teased her brown curls into an enchanting bundle behind her ears and had put together a modest headpiece, using some of the silk sample and a few cream-coloured feathers to achieve a delightful effect. When she presented herself to Henry, she almost took his breath away. "Jane, I've always thought you to be quite attractive, but may I say that you look absolutely charming in that outfit. If you're not careful, the Prince Regent will be wanting you to join his harem!"

"Don't be silly, Henry," she replied, but as she looked in the full-length mirror in the foyer, she had to agree it had been a long time since she had looked quite so fine.

"And I have another little surprise for you, Jane," replied Henry, picking up a rectangular box on the foyer table. "These are some of my treasured mementos of dear Eliza," he stated, pulling out a soft, cream-coloured shawl of wool and silk and a pair of cream kid gloves. "We don't want you catching a chill in this late-Autumn weather, do we," he exclaimed, handing her the gloves and putting the shawl around her shoulders.

"Oh, Henry, it is so thoughtful of you to let me borrow these," she replied, her eyes welling up with tears. "The day is so damp and grey, and it was making me feel a little chilled," she said against Henry's chest, as he gently held her until the emotion passed.

"*C'est si bon, ma petite*," Madame Bigeon clucked her approval, kissing her on both cheeks. Jane lifted her head and smiled warmly at them both. "I am so blessed," she murmured and pulled on the gloves. Thus fortified physically and emotionally, Jane departed with that venerable lady for her appointment at the London town mansion of the presiding British monarch!

They arrived unscathed at the portico of Carlton House on Pall Mall, and Jane and her *chaperone* were helped down from the carriage by the attendant in royal livery on duty. Jane gathered her skirts to ascend the steps to the massive door and managed to manoeuvre herself up the flight without incident. The door was opened noiselessly by another servant, who ushered them into the Grand Hall. Another servant, also in full livery, went in search of Rev. Clarke, while Jane and her companion moved toward chairs placed near the marble fireplace. As they sat, gazing in wonder at all the coloured marble in the room, Madame Bigeon expressed her desire to remain there by the fire while Jane toured the Library and other apartments. Jane thought to try and dissuade her, for she was loathe to be on her own in a strange situation, but she knew better than to argue with the firm-minded Frenchwoman. At that point, Rev. Clarke appeared, and there was no choice but to go forward on her own.

Rev. Clarke met them with a deep bow and immediately began to treat Jane like an old friend: "My dear Miss Austen, what a pleasure it is to have you here in this grand abode, and may I say how lovely you look this afternoon."

"Thank you, Rev. Clarke; I hope I have not taken you from something of great importance?" she inquired.

"No, " he replied, "although I was just showing Mr. William Wilberforce into an audience with the Prince Regent. A very interesting fellow—have you met him at all, Miss Austen?"

"Why, yes, he and his wife, Barbara Spooner, were married in Bath while we were on a visit before we went to live there. It was one of the most noteworthy celebrations of that city, for he was such a well-known Member of Parliament. And he was a near neighbour while my father was still living, and we made his acquaintance. He visited us in Sydney Place a number of times, and we met with him and his wife at concerts in Sydney Gardens, she replied, wondering a little at how comfortable she felt conversing with him.

"Really! How fortunate," he remarked.

"My brother, Henry, admires him greatly and has been on friendly terms with him through our cousin, Edward Cooper. My cousin is an Evangelical clergyman, and has met Mr. Wilberforce quite often at Rev. Gisborne's Yoxall Lodge in the Midlands." Jane was still pleasantly surprised at how easily the words tumbled out, considering her nervousness, but at least she wasn't standing there speechless, as she had dreaded.

"As a matter of fact," Rev. Clarke continued in a confidential tone, "I believe Mr. Wilberforce is going to sing for him this afternoon, for the Prince Regent has said he would go anywhere to hear the man sing! So this is a command performance for our fine friend," he concluded importantly.

Leaving Madame Bigeon by the fire with the tea he had ordered for her, Rev. Clarke led Jane down the ornate semicircular staircase, through the colourful Vestibule that led to the Library on the lower floor. Jane was immediately struck by the Gothic shelving that ornamented one side and the five large windows along the other. After she had perused the shelves for a few moments, remarking on the beautiful leather bindings on the various sets of books, she walked toward the windows and gazed out into the large walled garden that stretched away down the Mall. "What a lovely setting, she murmured to herself," feeling a little like her heroine, Lizzy, at Mr. Darcy's Pemberley estate in *Pride and Prejudice*.

Rev. Clarke had left her momentarily to go to a particular corner of the room. He returned triumphantly, carrying a number of books in his arms. "You see, Miss Austen, how fond the Prince Regent is of your novels. Just look at the binding and gold lettering on these volumes of *Sense and Sensibility, Pride and Prejudice, and Mansfield Park*—all by an anonymous lady!" he beamed.

Jane reddened slightly and tried to appear nonchalant, but she had to admit she never expected to see her master-pieces in this magnificent setting. "Why, I must admit I am a little overwhelmed at the idea of their being here," she stammered.

"And, of course, the Prince Regent has beautifully bound copies in his other palaces as well. In fact, he has given them as gifts to his sisters, the princesses. And the Queen, his mother, also admires them and feels they are having a real moral influence on the country. You should be very proud of your work, Miss Austen," he concluded.

"I had no idea they had found their way to such exalted circles," Jane retorted lamely. How quickly her conversa-tional competence had dissipated! Why did she always find it confusing and difficult to express herself when the focus was on her? She was beginning to wish she were a million miles away from this place at the moment!

Rev. Clarke seemed not to notice, and presumed she was savouring the sumptuousness of the room. After a suit-able passage of time he led her through the doors at one end into the adjoining magnificent Drawing Room. There were gold Corinthian pillars and large mirrors, reflecting light throughout the room, and the grandeur completely took Jane's breath away. Rev. Clarke carried on, in the manner of Mr. Collins, citing statistics about the number of pillars and vases and fireplaces in Carlton House, pointing out a special *objet d'art* here and a gift from some foreign prince there. Jane did her best to concentrate, but after just two rooms, she was beginning to be weary.

Having slowly traversed the length of the Drawing Room, the Chaplain/Librarian led her on into a Gothic Dining Room, which was unlike anything Jane had ever seen in her life. As she gazed up at its soaring arches, she thought wryly that her little heroine, Catherine, in a novel she had not yet published would surely fall over in a dead faint in this room! "Yes, there is material here to embellish that plot," she mused silently. Of Rev. Clarke, she inquired, "Was this the room in which there was an indoor fountain and an artificial brook that ran down the centre of the table?"

Rev. Clarke was obviously pleased that she had heard of the Carlton House Fete on the occasion of the Prince being named Regent in 1811. "In this very room, dear Madam, with an extraordinary number of notables in attendance, and, of course, I was pleased to be present on that impressive occasion!" he replied.

There was a bustle of servants at the far end of the room, and they walked in that direction. Rev. Clarke had arranged for tea to be brought to a small table in a corner of the room, and Jane was very grateful to be able to sit down and partake of some refreshment. She thought, rather sardonically, that it was "fit for a king" as she consumed several of the delicious pastries. Walking through these rooms, even at such a leisurely pace, had worked up an appetite. The Librarian continued chattering during teatime, and Jane found she needed to contribute very little to the conversation. He was happy to have such an attentive audience, and she had to confess he had many interesting tales to tell.

The Chaplain/Librarian offered to show her more of the grand rooms, saying, "There are magnificent collections of paintings, ceramics, and gilded silver you haven't seen yet." But hastily she assured him she had seen sufficient to satisfy her, and she must get back to Madame Bigeon and Henry. He led her back up the ornate staircase to the the place they had left her companion. The older lady seemed pleased, if somewhat impatient, to see her again, and shortly thereafter they bade Rev. Clarke adieu.

"Do not forget to ensure that your publisher includes the dedication to the Prince Regent in your next novel," was his parting shot. Jane curtseyed her acknowledgement and retreated into the comfort of Henry's barouche.

Rev. Clarke returned to retrieve William Wilberforce and show him back to the grand entrance. The Prince Regent requested that he come back for some conversation as soon as he was finished with that task, and Rev. Clarke was quick to respond.

"Well, Clarke, how did you find Miss Austen this afternoon?" was his immediate question.

"Very charming indeed, your Highness, and quite attractively *accoutred*, I must say. But perhaps a little hesitant and reticent to put herself forward, as such a successful novelist might be expected to" was his reply.

"Well, well—not suitable for any little liaisons at Carlton House then, I presume, heh, heh!" the Prince remarked, laughing at the thought.

"No, your Highness, I don't believe so. As you can tell from the subject matter of her novels, she is a rather morally upright lady—and not married," he added, significantly.

"Just so, just so. Pity, though. We can always use fresh female company," he remarked, rising from the comfortable gilded chair in which he was lounging. "But maybe she would be suitable for a single man-of-the-cloth like you, Clarke," he added.

"I suppose she is about ten years younger than I, and she would be eminently suitable as a clergyman's wife. But I believe I prefer someone a little more outgoing than Miss Jane Austen—although she certainly has pristine literary tastes," he mused. "I may just keep up a correspondence with her and see what develops."

"Har, har, har, way to go Clarke, way to go," replied the Prince Regent. Rev. Clarke seemed lost in thought for a moment, so His Royal Highness continued, "That Wilberforce fellow is quite remarkable, you know. He's one of the wittiest people I've ever met! And his voice is even better than I expected—quite lyrical, really, and pleasing tonal quality for someone his age.

"And what did he sing for you, Sir?" inquired Rev. Clarke.

"Why, the rascal insisted on singing *Amazing Grace!* He said that old slaver, John Newton, wrote it. I didn't stop him, though I had a mind to. It seems the Evangelicals are making that song the latest rage of the whole kingdom. I don't know what we're coming to in this realm if everybody's singing that kind of rubbish! 'That saved a wretch like me' indeed— such poppycock for Wilberforce to think he's a wretch! He may admit to it, but I certainly will not. I hope you don't go around singing lyrics of that nature, Clarke!

"No, your Highness, I tend to be more familiar with the Anglican Liturgy," he replied, smiling.

"And as Chaplain to my Household, so you should be!" retorted the Prince Regent grandly, waving him out of the room.

Meanwhile, the celebrated authoress, Jane Austen, leaned back into the comfortable, cushioned interior of Henry's carriage, thoroughly drained by the afternoon's experience. She was so relieved to be heading toward a more familiar place where she could feel at home with her thoughts again. How much she would have to share with Henry—perhaps tomorrow when she was feeling more rested, for the experience had tired her more than she would have imagined. She might have enough energy left to write to James' son, James Edward, later this evening. He would be amazed at how prescient was the poem he had written not too long ago concerning his Aunt Jane!

Chapter 4

A Letter to
James Edward Austen

23 Hans Place, London

My dear James Edward,

You will never guess how your doting Aunt has been occupied this day! You will doubtless recall that excellent poem you wrote and sent to me when you first found out I was the author of *Sense and Sensibility* and *Pride and Prejudice*? I am going to quote it here, in case you've forgotten some of the lines, and to show you that your Aunt Jane was so impressed with it that she actually memorised it!

No words can express, my dear Aunt, my surprise
 Or make you conceive how I opened my eyes,
Like a pig Butcher Pile has just struck with his knife,
 When I heard for the very first time in my life
That I had the honour to have a relation
 Whose works were dispersed throughout the whole
 of the nation.
I assure you, however, I'm terribly glad;
 Oh dear! just to think (and the thought drives me
 mad)

> *That you made the Middletons, Dashwoods, and all,*
>   *And that you (not young Ferrars) found out that*
>   *a ball*
> *May be given in cottages never so small.*
>   *And though Mr. Collins, so grateful for all,*
> *Will Lady de Bourgh his dear Patroness call,*
>   *'Tis to your ingenuity he really owed*
> *His living, his wife, and his humble abode.*

I trust you are taking every opportunity to put your pen to paper to produce more of these rollicking poems, for they bring such pleasure to your "relations." Indeed your poem has proved prophetic, for as a matter of fact it turns out that your relation's works are being dispersed throughout the whole of the nation!

I confess I had no idea that the scribblings I began in my younger years would culminate in novels that are being read by members of the royal family! And just how did I discover this, you ask? Well, dear boy, during your Uncle Henry's recent serious illness, he couldn't restrain himself from telling his doctor, who is also the Prince Regent's physician, that his sister is the authoress of *Sense and Sensibility, Pride and Prejudice*, and *Mansfield Park*.

I'm afraid your Uncle opened a Pandora's Box for your Aunt Jane, because shortly thereafter I received a visit from the Prince Regent's Chaplain and Librarian, Rev. James Stanier Clarke, inviting me to tour Carlton House Palace. Now I know you think Mr. Collins in *Pride and Prejudice* is a unique result of my ingenuity, but if you had met Rev. Clarke, you would think that Mr. Collins had a twin! As you are doubtless aware, I take great pains to make sure that my fictional characters are unlike any particular person I know or have ever met. It is unbelievable, then, that this man mimics this figment of my imagination as if he had come from the same womb as Mr. Collins. And, truly, he is amazing to behold when he begins his sweeping gestures and obsequious bows, and you hear the way he talks, using such florid language. I'm sure if you met him you would agree that it would be far better if he were more like the young Mr. Edward Ferrars.

But I haven't told you the most interesting part of the story, for today your Aunt Jane was a guest of the Prince Regent at Carlton House in London! Henry bought me a new dress, so that I wouldn't embarrass the Austen name by appearing in less than London's highest fashion. And I arrived in Henry's coach, feeling a little like Cinderella, visiting the prince's palace. I was glad to hear that the Prince Regent (you are well aware of my feelings concerning him!) was busy entertaining Mr. Wilberforce at the time—or, rather, Mr. Wilberforce was more likely entertaining him.

Mr. Clarke took great pains to show me around the magnificent interiors, and he sounded so like Mr. Collins in describing them that I had to struggle to retain my composure. We only had time to see the Library, the Gold Drawing Room, and the Gothic Dining Room, but any one of them would have taken your breath away. It is a shame to see so much money wasted on such opulence when the poor people of our country live in hovels and have so little to eat. What was most amazing to me was to see beautifully bound volumes of my three novels—showing suitable signs of wear and tear—on the Prince Regent's shelves. Mr. Clarke assured me that there are sets in each of his palaces and that his sisters, the princesses, are reading them as well!

Well, your Aunt Jane just couldn't wait to share such interesting news with you. And I want to encourage you that your literary efforts are not in vain—that you have been the means of bringing me and others in your family much pleasure. I have always enjoyed your strong, manly, spirited sketches, full of variety and glow, so different from my much more delicate and laborious attempts.

I strongly feel than an author should stimulate people to supply what is not obvious, take trivial scenes and form them into the stuff of which life is made. In the process, you must make sure you stress character and the development of it, enduing your characters with the right degree of admiration. As an architect and narrator of fiction, your plots and characters should be suitable and sensible.

Your writing should be unique, according to your own gifting—as distinctive perhaps as Sir Walter Scott's may be from mine. Be sure your novels are values-laden, with your characters discriminating right from wrong, better from worse, improving in their development. As they evaluate and discriminate, allow their speech to mirror their inner reflections. Take your various strands of plot and weave them together toward a tight pattern of wholeness and completion that will bring the readers real satisfaction.

To conclude, my dear nephew, if my efforts are gaining some recognition, I hope that will provide you with some incentive to pursue the literary gifts with which you appear to be blessed. Some day, in the not-too-distant future we may be reading ingenious books of poetry and prose penned by none other than my honoured relation, James Edward Austen!

Until then, I remain your affectionate aunt,
J. Austen

Chapter 5

A Hopeful New Year

J ane arrived downstairs for breakfast just as Henry was finishing his. She had been so tired from her previous afternoon's exertions that she had over-slept—unusual for such an early riser who usually practiced at the pianoforte an hour before breakfast. "Sorry, Henry," you should have wakened me earlier," she began somewhat sleepily, smothering a yawn.

"I hadn't the heart, Jane. You deserve the luxury of over-sleeping once in awhile," he replied pleasantly. "But now that you're here, I want to hear all about your tour of the Prince Regent's palace," he continued, pouring himself another cup of coffee from the sideboard.

"Why, it was all very grand," she began, "so much so that I hardly know where to begin. It was rather ostentatious, really, with a strange mixture of styles, as is his palace at Brighton, I understand. I suppose it's largely neoclassical, but certainly has an admixture of Gothic and Chinese as well. I saw only three rooms in detail, and I suppose my favourite must be the Library. Mr. Clarke sounded a lot like Mr. Collins, as he showed me around, but you can be sure I suppressed my mirth as best I could," she concluded, noting that he was grinning at her like a Cheshire cat!

"Well, I told you such a visit would give you more material for another novel, didn't I?" he retorted.

"Yes, I imagine I can spice up my novel about Catherine and her fascination with the Gothic novel, just from what I saw in the Dining Room there," she replied. "At any rate, it is true the Prince Regent has all three sets of my novels there, for Mr. Clarke pulled them from the shelves and showed them to me. They had signs of wear and tear, too," she added.

"Maybe your moral tales will do him some good in the long run, Jane," suggested Henry, smiling.

"I'm not sure they will, but Mr. Wilberforce had an audience with him during the time I was on my tour, so perhaps he will have a stronger influence than I," she replied.

"Well, I was wondering how my old friend, Wilber, is. I think he's beginning to show his age, largely from the toll his anti-slavery campaign took over the years. But I imagine raising six children is stressful as well—not that either of us would know much about that," he concluded.

The mail that morning brought two letters—one for Henry and one for our favourite novelist. Madame Bigeon handed her the thicker of the two, franked from Carlton House, and in the process dropped her a little curtsey.

"Now, Madame, don't start that," she reprimanded her gently. "I'm not the least bit altered since being invited to Carlton House, and I'll thank you to treat me as the poor, unknown authoress that I am for some time to come," she retorted, laughing over her shoulder as she retreated to the Sitting Room to read the contents of her letter. It was from Rev. Clarke, of course, and she was surprised that it had come so soon after her visit. But she had not read far before she went in search of Henry to share the contents with him.

"Henry, you will never believe what nonsense Mr. Clarke is writing to me," she began. He is offering me the use of his personal library and his apartments in Golden Square, should I need them while he is away. Can you imagine—the impropriety of the very thought!" she trailed off.

"Well, Jane, he is a man about the Court—a very liberal Court, as we both know—and he probably thinks it very kind to make you the offer. Perhaps this bachelor clergyman has as great an interest in you as in your writings, my sweet sister," Henry replied.

"Perish the thought! I could never be attracted to someone with his pomposity. He is full of such strange ideas. He is importuning me to write a novel about a literate clergyman like himself—more distinguished than Mr. Collins (can you believe it?)—a man whose time is divided between the country and the city. He even suggests I carry him to sea as the friend of a distinguished naval character. And he also wants me to deal with the issue of tythes and of his burying his own mother, if you please!" she concluded incredulously. "I shall decline, of course, to undertake such a foolhardy project. And, he concludes by reiterating his permission to dedicate *Emma* to the Prince Regent," she ended hopelessly. "Henry, I feel I must write Rev. Clarke to clarify whether it is incumbent upon me to do this dedication. I am still not comfortable with the thought. What an insufferable association it entails," she stated a little too warmly.

"My dear sister, I don't believe you'll have any choice in the matter. But, if it will put your mind at ease, do write to him and get clarification concerning the dedication."

"I believe I shall, just so that I can have some peace of mind about this. As you are aware, my writing is very important to me, Henry; in fact, it is becoming my very life. *Emma* is ready to be printed, and it is giving me great unease to have this situation so unsettled. I'm afraid this Court visit is leading to more trouble than I expected."

"Now, Jane, no catastrophising is necessary on this point. Communicate with Rev. Clarke, and he will help you to solve it in one way or another."

"You're right, of course, Henry—as usual. I will ask for his opinion concerning it right away. Thank you for your wise counsel. What would I ever do without you!" she finished, looking intently into his face.

"Well, Jane, I think you're going to have to do without me for awhile," he responded, rather soberly. "The banking business is in a serious state of flux, and I fear I must be off to Alton to deal with some situations that have arisen there. My illness has kept me out of the flow of things for awhile, and there are dire consequences ahead if I do not become involved immediately."

"Oh, dear, Henry!" she replied. "What do you propose?"

"I suggest our returning to Chawton in the next week. Christmas will soon be upon us, and I know your mother and Cassandra and Martha would be pleased to have you back with them to help in the preparations," he responded. I will plan to stay there for Christmas, if all are in agreement," he concluded.

"I can be packed as soon as you wish to leave, Henry," she replied, "but there is one thing I would like to do before we leave London—and that is a visit to our brother Charles' three little girls in Keppel Street. I know their grandparents and aunt Harriett are doing their utmost to make up for the loss of their mother, but I feel a particular burden for them and want to see how they're doing for myself," she said, a little wistfully.

"I'm glad you mentioned it, Jane, for I have just had a letter from Charles informing me that he is on leave and is visiting his girls in Keppel Street this very week," he stated in a pleased tone.

"Oh, how perfect, Henry! I have been longing to see Charles again, and to see him reunited with those precious little girls will be such a pleasure," she exclaimed.

"Shall we visit them tomorrow and leave the day after next, then?" he inquired of her.

"I'll be ready," she said, feeling a stir of excitement at returning to her beloved Hampshire.

Their visit with Charles and his in-laws was a delightful one indeed, for the little ones crowded around their Aunt Jane, and she responded by telling them story after story until she was quite tired out.

After a refreshing afternoon tea, Henry and Jane took their leave, urging Charles to join them for New Year celebrations at Chawton if he possibly could. As they drove back to Hans Place in Henry's curricle on that sunny afternoon, Jane remarked that she thought Charles was showing a more-than-brother-in-law interest in Harriett, his deceased wife's sister. Henry assured her she was probably imagining something that didn't exist, but Jane felt sure that her intuition was telling her about a romance developing there!

When they arrived back at Hans Place, there was a letter from Rev. Clarke for Jane. She looked at Henry ruefully as she opened the seal, knowing that it could contain news she did not want to hear. "I asked him if it was incumbent on me to show my sense of the honour by dedicating my forthcoming novel to His Royal Highness, Henry, and this is his answer: 'It is certainly not incumbent on you, but if you wish to do the Regent that honour either now or at any future period, I am happy to send you that permission which need not require any more trouble or solicitation on your part.'"

"I think that can be interpreted as giving you little choice in the matter, Jane," replied Henry. "It is what is known in Court circles as a command performance. If you refuse, you will be seen as being unwilling to honour the Prince Regent. I think you had better transmit the information to Mr. Murray in Albermarle Street right away!"

The next day they departed for Chawton, leaving their beloved Frenchwomen with kisses on each cheek several times over and promising they would both be back as early in the new year as they could.

The drive to Hampshire in Henry's barouche was a little fatiguing for both, and they were glad to be welcomed around a warm fire at the former bailiff's cottage that Edward had made available to his mother and sisters. Cassandra embraced Jane with all the warmth of her nurturing capability and cheered her sister considerably in the process. Their mother gave Jane a quick hug and then clung to Henry for a few moments, realising that he had had a close brush with death and had almost been taken from her.

Henry was off the next morning to Alton, leaving Jane with Cassandra and Martha to catch up on all the news of the neighbourhood. It seemed they couldn't have enough of each others' company, so compatible were these three middle-aged women. Mrs. Austen lay on the couch a good deal of the time, while they searched through the attic, pulling out neat boxes of ornaments for the fresh tree Henry promised to bring home that afternoon. Martha talked of the new Christmas recipes she had discovered and added to her cookbook. Jane had to admit it was good to be home again with family and friends in familiar surroundings!

They celebrated her birthday on December 16th with a special cake Martha prepared for the occasion. Jane didn't want to have any kind of fuss, but since this was her fortieth birthday, she couldn't do much to prevent the celebration. She was pleased with the French wine from Henry, the silk stockings from Cassandra and Martha, and the new lace cap from her mother, and was grateful that they had not invited anyone else. She preferred to not draw the attention of the world to this milestone in her life.

Christmas Eve was indeed a special time for the household, as they all attended the usual candlelight service at St. Nicholas Church, Chawton. The women wrapped up Mrs. Austen warmly against the cold, and Henry made sure there were glowing bricks in his barouche. On such an occasion, they all missed Mr. Austen, but tried not to let it affect their appreciation of the occasion. Henry had been asked to read the age-old Christmas story from the book of Luke, and Jane was pleased to note that his voice was stronger than it had been for a long time. He would make a very good clergyman, she thought, as he returned from the pulpit to take his place beside her.

The next day was all Jane could have wanted, for after opening gifts in the morning, her brother, James, and his wife and three children joined them for Christmas dinner. Having ten around the table was a special treat for all, and Jane couldn't help but marvel at how grown up her brother's children were. It seemed they had developed overnight, although Anna's high spirits were still very much in evidence! James Edward was becoming quite an affable and mature young man, and Caroline was as whimsical and romantically idealistic as ever. Jane thought that she must have been a lot like Caroline when she was her age.

After the dinner dishes had been cleared, Jane found a few moments with her eldest brother, for she wanted to discuss with him the literary potential she was observing in his children. James, as easy-going as ever, was glad to sit with her and engage in conversation. "James, as I spend time with your family, I have been reminiscing about how much of myself I see in them. Do you remember my being as romantic as your Caroline when I was younger?"

"It is strange that you should ask, Jane, for I was telling Mary the other day how much like Caroline you were as a child. In fact, I think you were that way until after you moved to Bath at the age of twenty-five! And, having read your novels, I am not sure you have changed," he grinned. "I remember we all thought you were a hopeless romantic when you reversed your decision to marry Harrison Bigg-Wither because you declared you weren't in love with him. But I suppose Cassandra was always the practical sister, and you were the sentimental idealist. I'm not sure you have altered very much over the years," he remonstrated.

"Oh, James," said Jane, laughing, "you never were one to hold back the truth. Do you really perceive me in that way today?"

"I suppose you have become more mature in forty years, but you are still such a contrast with your sister," he replied.

"Yes, I can't fault your judgment in that regard, but I've never been as emotionally volatile as your Anna, have I?" she queried, smiling at him.

"No, I don't know anyone who is as explosive as she is when it comes to feelings. She is rather like a volcano, really, ready to erupt at any time. But I suppose a lot of that can be attributed to the loss of her mother at an early age and the insecurity she experienced then," he responded.

"I think you might be right," replied Jane, "but I certainly see much literary potential in both of them, and your dear James Edward. Of course, you have mentored them and nurtured their talent in much the same way you did for me as a child. And I want you to know how grateful I am for that, James. I wouldn't be the author of four published novels now if it hadn't been for your patience and help in my formative years," she concluded.

"I'm glad I could be of such use to you, Jane, but our father and Henry also had a hand in that, as I'm well aware," he replied.

"That is true, but I want to return the favour to your children by helping to develop their literary abilities, if you do not think that is presuming too much, brother," Jane responded seriously.

"I would be more than pleased for you to do that, Jane, for all your siblings agree that you are the literary star in this family. If my children have half your success in that regard, I would be delighted," he replied pleasantly.

"Thank you, James. It helps me feel fulfilled that I can make some contribution to the next generation, since I don't have any children of my own to nurture in that way. I have always felt very close to your three and want to be a good aunt to them all," she said, looking quite earnest.

"They all esteem you very highly and will be grateful for any attention you show them," he said, patting her on the knee and rising to go back to the fireside where his mother was warming herself.

James had always been the most serious of her siblings and seemed more attached to his mother than any of the others. He was forever dropping in on them from Steventon at the most unexpected times. She wondered how much his Mary appreciated that, as she watched him conversing easily with their mother, their heads close together as they basked in the warm glow of the fire. James had few vices, and was a responsible Rector to the people of his parish. He would never be quite as capable in that regard as her father, but then there were few who could measure up to his stature," she thought to herself a little nostalgically.

On Boxing Day Jane felt more tired than she wanted to admit and was a little late getting the breakfast together—her particular responsibility in the household.

"I didn't hear the sounds of the pianoforte this morning," her mother remarked as she tried to manoeuvre her toast around some missing teeth.

"Yes, I must get back into the habit," Jane replied, feeling a little chagrined. Why was it her mother could make her feel so small with so little effort? It seemed to Jane it had always been that way since she was a young child. She must really exert herself to get over that feeling, and she was quite annoyed with herself that she had not yet conquered it—at the ripe age of forty! But she would make sure she was at the pianoforte early the next morning and that the breakfast was on the table at the expected time.

The next day Cassandra suggested to Martha and Jane that they walk in to Alton and buy a few things at the market there. Jane hesitated just long enough to stir her sister's curiosity, for Jane had always considered herself a "desperate walker."

"Perhaps I could ride to Alton with Henry this morning and walk back with you," she suggested, realising she was raising some concerns. Noting raised eyebrows, she continued, "I have found myself a little fatigued since Henry's illness, and I find I must conserve my energies rather more than hitherto. And besides, I'm forty now and deserve some consideration!" she exclaimed, trying to inject a little levity into the conversation.

The plan went forward as Jane had presented it, but that did not prevent Cassandra and Martha from discussing the situation on their way to Alton together. "I'm a little concerned about your sister, Cassandra," began Martha. "This is so unlike the Jane we have known so well," she concluded.

Cassandra tried not to let a note of worry creep into her voice as she replied, "I think perhaps she is still recovering from nursing Henry, Martha. I saw when I arrived in London what a great strain that had been on her. But let's keep a close eye on her and discuss this again if we see she isn't improving after the new year." Martha felt that was a wise suggestion, and they stopped at Henry's bank for Jane to join them and walk the mile or so back to Chawton. Jane went with them cheerfully and made a creditable effort in keeping up with their moderate pace as they walked together in the warm afternoon sun. They remarked on the unusually mild December that they were experiencing—so desirable after the gloomy November that year.

New Year's Eve arrived, and Charles was true to his word in arriving at the cottage earlier that afternoon. His cheerful countenance was always welcome in this household, and it was a while before he could take a break from all the questions with which they plied him concerning his latest adventures at sea. Jane watched him with an animated expression on her face. Her particular little brother, Charles, was as delightful as Henry in his own way. He had a boyish face and a grin that was immediately winsome. The relaxed curls on his forehead typified his easygoing personality that endeared him to everyone he met. She could well believe that the crews on his ships held him in high esteem, for he was always interested in the welfare of his men and their families. He was generous to a fault and insisted on spending his prize money on gifts for his family members. He had given her and Cassandra topaz crosses which they both would treasure for the rest of their lives.

She had not seen as much of him as she would have wished. At the age of twelve he had joined his older brother, Francis—Frank to their family—at the Naval College in Portsmouth. They had both gone to sea when they were fourteen and learned the ropes that enabled them to climb the laborious ladder that led to higher-ranking positions—never an easy task. He had spent five years in Bermuda, where he had met his pleasant blonde wife, Fanny Palmer. It was so sad that he had lost her in childbirth with their fourth child. Jane knew he must have lingering thoughts that if she had been on land, instead of his ship, at the time, she and the baby might have lived. It must be a struggle for him to leave his three children with his parents-in-law whenever he was at sea. But Charles never complained about anything. She was so happy to have him with them, even if it wasn't for long.

That evening they sat around the fire, reminiscing about their early family life at Steventon. They laughed about the performances in the barn every Christmas, remembering when Eliza had come from France to join them the first time. And how James and Henry had both fallen madly in love with her from that moment, and vied for her attentions after she was made a widow by the French guillotine.

"Well, I must say the best man won!" Henry exclaimed, and Jane was pleased to see he could bear talking about his dear, departed Eliza. He was one to always look on the positive side of life, with a constant cheerfulness that she envied.

Later in the evening, Henry produced a bottle of champagne he had procured in London for the occasion, and poured a small glass of the unaccustomed beverage for each. Charles was the first on his feet at midnight to propose a toast to "better health in the new year for everyone in the family." Henry said "Amen" to that, and so said they all! They parted shortly thereafter, agreeing that they would all sleep late, and Jane could be an hour later than usual preparing breakfast. She smiled her appreciation, and wended her way wearily up the steps to the bedroom she shared with Cassandra. "I do not enjoy late nights anymore," she commented, "but I suppose I should not mind just one night in the year." Cassandra looked at her searchingly, but decided wisely to leave a longer conversation about her health to another time when she wasn't so exhausted.

Jane amused herself by working on her "clergyman fragment" through the long Winter days, sitting at her little writing desk in the dining parlour of the house. This particular task did not come easily, for she had no desire to make a clergyman the central figure of any work. Perhaps it was because she was surrounded by so many clergymen in her extended family. Or maybe it was because she had a picture of Rev. Clarke in her mind every time she began to work on it! At least she no longer had to worry about the creaking door warning her of someone's approach, for the whole household knew of her authorship now. Somehow it felt good to have her writing activity out in the open and not a secret any more. And now she wouldn't be startled into stuffing her pages under the blotter, pretending to be nonchalant about the whole affair.

January was a much colder month, with wild winds rattling the windows of their comfortable cottage. She was glad she had the excuse of the weather to not have to walk very much, for she had periods of weakness and a lack of stamina that surprised her. Her lower back seemed to ache on both sides for some reason, and she was going to bed earlier at night. She had even put aside her writing for a time and placed three chairs together in the living room, in order to lie down and rest her fatigued body. Cassandra watched this, with increasing concern, but did not want to cause her sister any alarm, and so kept silent.

Toward the end of that month, Jane noticed the days growing longer and was hopeful that Spring would not be too far off. In mid-February the snowdrops and crocuses appeared, further cheering her disposition. Then the daffodils covered the lawn, "tossing their heads in sprightly dance," as Wordsworth had so aptly described their performance. The tulips appeared not long after that, for Jane's mother was still an avid gardener, when the weather was pleasant, and the results of her labour of love in their extensive garden were evident.

Jane felt herself returning more to normal and began to go out and about as the warm weather returned. She loved the Spring season and the riot of colour that nature indulged in at that time of the year. She absentmindedly wondered how Henry's garden was progressing, and suddenly realised that she was missing him more than she had anticipated. His intuitive understanding of her led to serious conversations on more wide-ranging topics than she could have with any other member of her family. She was close to Cassandra—had been all her life—but she somehow had a deeper relationship with Henry and now found herself longing for his cheerful company once more.

As if Henry had been privy to her thoughts, the next day a letter arrived for her from 23 Hans Place. His playful banter throughout lifted her spirits, and when he reported that Mr. Murray was ready to print a second edition of *Emma*, her joy knew no bounds. That the first edition should sell out so quickly gratified her immensely, and she knew she must go to London to check the proofs and make a few minor changes in the new edition.

Henry suggested as much and recommended he come to Chawton to collect her and Cassandra any day that week. That he would also invite Cassandra made his invitation doubly welcome, and she went quickly to find her sister to share with her the good news. Cassandra was pleased to be invited and secretly glad to go with Jane to keep an eye on her. She seemed to have improved with the coming of Spring, but Cassandra was careful to note any details that might indicate a relapse in her health. Martha Lloyd was her usual willing self and agreed to watch over their mother during their absence, which they thought might last several weeks at most.

They replied by return post, and Henry arrived two days later, eager to transport his sisters to London to enjoy the delights of the season. Jane chattered happily to him on the way, remarking on the lovely shades of green as the Hampshire countryside gave way to the more built-up outskirts of the sprawling city. Madame Bigeon and her daughter were more than delighted to see them, and scurried around Jane and Cassandra, greeting them affectionately and scolding Jane for not returning sooner.

After a restful night, Jane awoke to the pleasant sensation of being in her brother's house and not having to rush her *toilette* to make the breakfast for everyone. She was quite happy to let Madame Bigeon do the honours. The three siblings enjoyed an ample breakfast and then sat in the warmth of the garden, relaxing in each others' company and conversation. How good it was to be together again without Henry's dreadful illness to deal with!

"So, what have you been writing since I saw you last, Jane?" Henry enquired.

"Well, I've actually revised and added some sections to my "Gothic" novel about Catherine, since my visit to Carlton House. I don't have a name for it yet, and I'm not sure it's complete either. I may have to work on a more satisfactory ending for it, but it is slowly getting to the point where I might feel I could release it to a publisher," she finished. Henry and Cassandra both laughed outright at that remark. "Now what are you two laughing about?" she inquired, rather indignantly.

"Dear Jane," Henry replied, checking his mirth, for he had no desire to upset her in the least, "you always seem to have a struggle feeling that your novels are complete. You would revise and trim and 'lop and crop,' as you call it, until the cows come home, before submitting anything to a publisher."

"I suppose I am somewhat of a perfectionist when it comes to my writing," she replied, a little sheepishly.

"Yes, you certainly are," Cassandra commented, "but we find that rather endearing in you, don't we, Henry?"

"Indeed, we do," he replied warmly, "and that's only one of the things we love about you, Jane!"

Such pleasant conversation was only interrupted by the arrival of the day's mail, and Henry was mildly surprised to receive a letter he was not expecting. "It's from our cousin, Edward Cooper," he remarked, after breaking the seal. Reading to the end of the letter without comment, he raised his head and looked amusedly at his sisters.

"Well?" prompted Cassandra, as he hesitated.

"Edward makes an interesting proposal," he commented, eyes twinkling, for he knew this would divert Jane. Their thorougly Evangelical cousin was certainly not her favourite!

"And just what does our flambouyant cousin propose?" she questioned, not knowing quite what to expect.

"Why, that since he is coming to London from the Midlands next week to meet with William Wilberforce about the newly established British and Foreign Bible Society, that he bring Wilber and his wife here for a little dinner party next Wednesday," stated Henry, rather pleased with the idea. "In fact, they are aware of my interest in that subject, and they've invited me to meet them and a few other people with similar interests the day before at Clapham. I believe that is something I won't want to miss."

"Well, as you wish, Henry, but isn't it rather impertinent of Edward to invite himself and Mr. and Mrs. Wilberforce to dine at your house?" Jane inquired a little too sweetly.

"He's free and easy with me, as you well know, Jane. And I'm sure that the next thing you're going to tell me is that you hope to be back in Chawton before that little dinner party takes place," he replied, with that sardonic grin of his.

"I have to admit that thought has crossed my mind already, but I believe I could put up with our obnoxious cousin's company in order to meet the great man and his wife again. He is certainly a fascinating conversationalist, as I recall from our days in Bath," she concluded.

"What about you, Cassandra?" Henry inquired.

"Of course, I'd love to be there, Henry," she replied. "It sounds an enjoyable evening to me. Perhaps I could help Madame Bigeon with the planning of the menu," she offered pleasantly.

"Thank you," replied Henry. "It will be a very little, but lively, dinner party. And we will certainly have stimulating conversation and entertainment, too, if I'm not mistaken. Let me see, that makes three men and three women—a well-balanced group," he mused.

"That's if you consider your cousin well-balanced," Jane parried immediately, always ready to sharpen her wits with Henry.

"Now, Jane, don't start," he advised in big-brotherly tones. Edward is a talented fellow and is well received in his parishes at Hamstall-Ridware and Yoxall. He has had three volumes of his sermons printed thus far—quite an achievement for any clergyman, I must say. Wilberforce thinks the world of him and has asked him to lead two of the sixty-five charitable organisations he has established during his parliamentary career. I think that's a tribute to Edward's ability and intrinsic worth," he concluded.

"Well, a little humility in him would go a long way," she replied, entirely unmoved.

Henry knew he would not win that battle in a matter of a few minutes and wisely steered the conversation in another direction. "What do you lovely ladies think you'll wear on the occasion?" he questioned.

"Well, I have brought along my "Court" dress, and I think it will do very well for the dinner party, for no one has seen it but you," she replied, remembering the plum silk with pleasure. "Cassandra, I saw you pack that pretty blue brocade that looks so well on you, so together I think we will look quite splendid," she said, a little smugly.

"Now, who is in need of a dose of humility?" Henry queried, with arched eyebrows.

They broke up laughing then, and Henry went in search of pen and paper to write to his cousin. Jane retreated to her room to finish up the "clergyman fragment" which she wanted to send to Anna soon. And Cassandra headed in the direction of the kitchen to chat with Madame Bigeon about the menu for the forthcoming dinner party.

The only wrinkle in the planning was that the next day they heard from Edward that he wanted to bring Fanny to visit them in London, as he had business to attend to in

Chawton. Hearing that her favourite aunts were in London, Fanny was most anxious to spend some time with them, as well as do some shopping in the big city. Edward couldn't refuse her anything, and was happy to make such a suggestion to his genial brother. Henry checked with his sisters, but he knew the answer already. He was well aware that they doted on their niece and would be more than pleased to have her company. Perhaps he could arrange a little theatre party during her stay to please them all!

"We now have seven for our little dinner party," Cassandra reminded Henry when he told her the news. "Is there another man you could add to the group to make it even?" she enquired of him. "Not that it matters to me," she said, "but I know in London those kinds of things are important."

"Perhaps the handsome Dr. Charles Haden, for Fanny's benefit, or Rev. James Clarke, for Jane's benefit, could be persuaded," he remarked, eyes twinkling.

"Henry, you're always scheming," replied Cassandra. "Jane has told me all about Rev. Clarke, and I can't imagine she would enjoy an evening in his company. Why, it would be like having Mr. Collins to dinner!" she stated incredulously.

"Let this be our little surprise for Jane, Cassandra," retorted Henry. I'll write to Mr. Haden first, and if he is otherwise engaged, I'll write to Rev. Clarke. Whoever is available will be our dinner guest for the evening. Either will provide sufficient conversation and keep things—shall we say—interesting!

"Always plotting, aren't you, Henry?" she replied, shaking her head.

"It's what I was born to do, Cassandra," was his lighthearted reply, as he went in search of writing paper yet another time.

At dinner that evening, Jane revealed that she was ready to send off the "clergyman fragment" to James' daughter,

Anna. "I believe it's very important to encourage the writing skills of our next generation, Henry. Anna and I have chatted and corresponded about novel-writing, and I have tried to give her some helpful advice concerning her characters. You may think it a little ridiculous, but this "clergyman fragment" is a concrete way for me to show her some plot development and characterisation," she said, in a serious tone of voice.

"That's wonderful, Jane. I highly applaud what you're doing," he responded. "By the way, have you read Sir Walter Scott's critique of your *Emma* in the latest edition of the *Quarterly Review*," he questioned?

"Why, no, Henry. Have you been keeping it from me all this time?" she asked, a little annoyed.

"Just listen to this," he said, ignoring her question: 'We... bestow no mean compliment upon the author of *Emma*, when we say that, keeping close to common incidents, and to such characters as occupy the ordinary walks of life, she has produced sketches of such spirit and originality, that we never miss the excitation which depends upon a narrative of uncommon events, arising from the consideration of minds, manners, and sentiments, greatly above our own. In this class she stands almost alone; for the scenes of Miss Edgeworth are laid in higher life, varied by more romantic incident, and by her remarkable power of embodying and illustrating national character.'

"What do you think of that, Jane? He thinks you are unique — in a class of your own," commented Henry, enthusiastically. Jane was speechless, so he carried on, quoting, 'But the author of *Emma* confines herself chiefly to the middling classes of society; her most distinguished characters do not rise greatly above well-bred country gentlemen and ladies; and those which are sketched with most originality and precision, belong to a class rather below that standard. The narrative of all her novels is composed of such common occurrences as may have fallen under the observation of most folks; and her *dramatis personae* conduct themselves upon the motives and principles which the readers may recognize as ruling their own and that of most of their acquaintances. The kind of moral, also, which these novels inculcate, applies equally to the paths of common life.'"

Jane seemed a little overwhelmed, so Henry rushed headlong into the silence, "I'm not saying this to flatter you—for I mean it sincerely—but everything you write, Jane, is of consequence, whether it be poetry or prose. Sir Walter Scott recognizes that your novels are instilling morals in their readers. And your nieces and nephews will one day be proud that they are so closely related to such a famous authoress— when they discover all that you've been writing so secretly!" he said, smiling.

"Well, I'm afraid they will find out soon enough, if you have anything to do with it, Henry. I just might have to tell them myself before you do" she retorted, excusing herself to go and finish the letter to Anna, and to ponder the words of such an eminent figure in the literary world.

Cassandra had been sitting back, sipping her coffee and grinning at her two siblings as they carried on in their own inimitable way. She didn't feel herself equal to their literary or intuitive powers, but she could certainly enjoy their good-natured bantering with one another. "I hope she'll share that "clergyman fragment" with us, Henry. It sounds fascinating," she offered.

"Well, we just may have a whole clergyman to share with her," replied Henry, that twinkle in his eyes again. "It seems Mr. Haden is otherwise engaged, and Rev. Clarke is coming to dinner!"

Chapter 6

A Letter to Anna Austen Lefroy

23 Hans Place, London

My dear budding authoress, Anna,

Your fond Aunt Jane has been thinking of you lately and wanted to enquire as to how you're getting along with the "three or four families in a country village" that we discussed in our last correspondence. I would be delighted to read anything you have written along that line, and beg you to let me hear about it at the first opportunity

I suppose you have heard from your brother by now that your dear Aunt Jane has been producing some novels of late that have clergymen as secondary characters. By now, I believe you will be familiar with Mr. Edward Ferrars, Mr. Collins, and Mr. Edmund Bertram? There's a Mr. Elton in circulation now, too, in case you haven't come across my latest, *Emma*. Can you believe, sweet Anna, that those clergymen are all figments of your Aunt Jane's imagination? And I hope they are stimulating enough to get your pen moving over the page, producing your own delightful portraits of characters in your turn.

I would advise you to endeavour to transport people out of assorted difficult circumstances in which they find themselves, and entertain them so well that they can scarcely find their way back to the real world, where so much unpleasantness abounds. But do leave them with an afterglow that helps them escape, oft and again, to that which might uplift them in manners and morals.

I have put together a few paragraphs that might entertain you with regard to a very interesting clergyman character. Unlike my other novels, this clergyman is a central character, patterned after someone I am coming to know very well. It strikes me, dear Anna, that men have had every advantage—education has been theirs in so much higher a degree—but the pen has been in their hands for too long! It is time that we women, armed with our writing instruments, had a strong moral influence in this world. After all, I have been scrambled into a little education at Steventon, Oxford, Southampton, and Reading, so it should be obvious to all that I am eminently qualified to write such novels! And if I can do it,dear Anna, so can you.

I would urge you to be an artist—but with your pen instead of your brush. Paint portraits of lords and ladies, gentlemen and gentlewomen, using broad and fine brush strokes to delineate their inner thoughts and feelings as well as their outward behaviours. Give them form and movement and texture, so that your end product is a harmonious whole.

I will be interested to have your comments when you have read the enclosed "fragment"—I have called it such because it can easily be enhanced and expanded if you think the plot and characters are appealing. The name of the work could be *Lucinda,* and I have tried to write it in the style of *Sense and Sensibility* and *Pride and Prejudice*, rather than *Emma.*

Finally, dearest Anna, I have penned this with no particular purpose other than that it be for your own particular pleasure. Please give my fond regards to that charming clergyman husband of yours!

Believe me your affectionate Aunt,
Jane

About fifty years ago, in a tiny village in the beautiful, rolling countryside of Hampshire, the Rev. Clarence Worthington Gilford, with a very small fortune of his own, settled into a comfortable curacy to spend the rest of his years in peace and tranquillity. His daughter, Lucinda, highly accomplished at twenty-one, but tender of heart and sentimental, accompanied him with great expectation to this parish, for she had longed for many years to be able to live in the verdant green countryside.

They were admirable companions for one another. She was accomplished in everything young ladies should learn, as well as understanding modern languages and excelling in singing and playing on the pianoforte and harp. And he was the most excellent of men, perfect in character, temper, and manners. Our heroine was quite faultless and beautiful, perfectly good, with dark eyes and plump cheeks, and her father was of a very literary turn, an enthusiast in literature, really, and nobody's enemy but his own. Rev. Gilford was the very model of an exemplary Parish Priest, very zealous in the discharge of his pastoral duties, and without the smallest peculiarity to prevent his being the most delightful companion to his daughter. With such noble accomplishments on either side, father and daughter were able to converse animatedly, from one year's end to another, in long speeches, elegant language, and a tone of high, serious sentiment!

Lucinda's father had lived much in the world, but was now glad to be retired from it, and equally delighted to have his daughter removed from circumstances where young suitors were always in attendance on her. He had done his best to shield her from the worst of them and now hoped they might both have some respite from the constant stream of young men who were vying for her attentions. Lucinda, to while away the Winter evenings, induced him through earnest pleading to relate to her the past events of his life. She desired that he include all the circumstances of his attachment to her mother, as well as their marriage, for that dear lady had been parted from her at birth owing to her death from childbed fever. Lucinda begged her father to relate the details of his going to sea as Chaplain to a rather distinguished naval character about the Court, and his going afterwards to Court himself, which introduced him to a great variety of characters and involved him in many interesting situations. She had heard only snippets of these amazing tales and was anxious to live them anew as her father related them in his own inimitable way.

In long, serious soliloquies he was also happy to share with her his opinion of the benefits to result from tythes being done away with, as he had expended much time and tribulation on trying to collect them when he was Rector of a large parish in East Sussex. He lamented at great length on having to bury his own mother (Lucinda's lamented grandmother) in consequence of the High Priest of the parish in which she died, refusing to pay her remains the respect he felt due to them. His daughter's heart was alternately rended and torn and soothed and consoled by these elegant speeches and noble sentiments, and she would sometimes be close to fainting on the sofa or swooning in a wild delirium, until they finally came to their conclusion in the early Spring.

As she was able to get out and about in the little village in which they had settled, Lucinda's friendship was sought after by a young woman in the same neighbourhood. Although this interesting creature had talents and shrewdness to recommend her, as well as light eyes and fair skin, our heroine shrank from encouraging the relationship, as the young woman had a considerable degree of wit, in which our heroine was lacking. And, if truth be told, Lucinda was, like many young ladies of her age, more interested in attracting the attention of young men of the surrounding countryside.

Fortunately, or unfortunately, it was not long before a handsome young clergyman named Horatio Tillerton, from the adjoining parish, came one morning to consult her father on some matters of mutual interest. Lucinda answered the knock on their cottage door and was immediately smitten by the young man. He, in turn, thought her quite ravishing, and proceeded to find excuses to visit her father as frequently as he could, without, of course, neglecting his parish duties. Her father took to the young man and would have encouraged his courtship of his daughter. But, alas—all perfection—this amiable would-be suitor was prevented from paying his addresses to her by an outmoded excess of refinement. In the meantime, a roguish young fellow fell desperately in love with Lucinda and began pursuing her with unrelenting passion. He was a totally unprincipled and heartless young man, who used his vile arts to drive our heroine's father from his curacy, when the latter would not permit the passionate suitor to court the lovely Lucinda.

Father and daughter fled to the Continent of Europe to escape the evil calumnies this young man spread concerning them. From this point forward they were involved in a striking variety of adventures and were never more than two weeks in any one place. No sooner had they settled in a town or city of one country than they were necessitated to quit it and retire to another—always making new acquaintances and always obliged to leave them. They met a wide variety of characters with seemingly no admixture of traits. The scene was forever shifting from one set of people to another, with all the good unexceptionable in every respect and having no foibles or weaknesses, and all the wicked being depraved and infamous with hardly a resemblance of humanity left in them.

Wherever Lucinda and her father went, somebody fell in love with her, and she received repeated offers of marriage— which she always referred wholly to her father. Indeed, she was exceedingly angry that he should not be first applied to! So unscrupulous in their behaviour were the young men of the Continent that Lucinda was often tricked into being carried away by them, only to be rescued by her father or the young Hampshire clergyman, Horatio, upon whom her father called when he had not the energy to find her himself. During this dreadful period of their history, our heroine was often reduced to supporting herself and her father by her talents, having to work for her bread. In fact, she was continually cheated and defrauded of her hire, worn down to a mere skeleton, and now and then starved almost to death.

At last, hunted out of civilized society and denied the poor shelter of the humblest cottage, they were compelled to retreat into Kamschatka. Here her poor father, quite worn down, finding his end approaching, finally threw himself on the ground. After four or five hours of tender advice and parental admonition to his miserable child, he expired in a fine burst of literary enthusiasm, intermingled with invectives against holders of tythes!

Our dear heroine was inconsolable for some time—but afterwards crawled back toward her former Hampshire countryside—having at least twenty narrow escapes of falling into the hands of the roguish young man who had caused her all this grief. In the very nick of time, turning a corner to avoid this odious rascal, she ran into the arms of her hero, the young clergyman himself. Horatio, having just shaken off the scruples which fettered him before, was at that very moment setting off in pursuit of her. The most tender and complete *eclaircissement* took place, and they were happily united. Throughout the whole of their long married life, Lucinda's character and accomplishments enabled her to move easily in the most elegant Hampshire society, and Horatio's promotions up the ecclesiastical ladder permitted them to live in a high style, of which her departed father would be justly proud!

Chapter 7

A Unique Dinner Party

The week of the dinner party arrived, and Edward brought Fanny to Hans place a couple of days before the event. Jane and Cassandra welcomed her with open arms, as did Henry, for it had been some time since they had seen their young niece. Henry pressed Edward to stay longer, but he was anxious to get to Chawton and left shortly after leaving his daughter with them. They all relaxed over a refreshing afternoon tea and talked excitedly of the plans for the exquisite evening dinner party. Fanny had never met Mr. Wilberforce and was suitably impressed that her Uncle Henry was a close friend of the famous Member of Parliament.

Cassandra and Fanny shopped together during the next day, while Jane saved her strength for the theatre that night. They all enjoyed it thoroughly and chatted animatedly about the actors and actresses over a late breakfast the next morning. Fanny added youthful enthusiasm to the conversation, and Henry was pleased to see them delighting in each other.

As the time for dinner approached, the three ladies helped put the finishing touches to one another's costumes. "Oh, Aunt Jane, you look so pretty in that plum colour; it suits your dark hair so well," exclaimed Fanny.

"Thank you for the compliment, my sweet niece, and you look rather ravishing in that delicate cream colour, with the lovely lace" replied Jane. "And doesn't Aunt Cass look wonderful in that beautiful shade of blue?"

"Methinks we may be the belles of the ball," Cassandra commented, twirling around and dropping a little curtsey to the other two. "But Mrs. Wilberforce may outshine us all, as I understand she is somewhat younger than her husband and still quite a beauty."

"Well, then, we shall make a delightful quartet, instead of a trio," stated Fanny, lifting her chin and smiling impudently. They all laughed delightedly and decided it was time to descend the staircase to be ready to receive the guests.

Henry met them at the bottom of the stairs, looking as handsome and dashing as ever, kissing each of their hands in turn. "You ladies take my breath away, and I'm sure you'll do the same for the other gentlemen in our party tonight," he remarked, laughing.

They heard the sound of a carriage outside and quickly scurried to sit demurely in the comfortable chairs in Henry's Sitting Room, while he went to the door to welcome his guests. A moment later he appeared, accompanied by Edward Cooper and Mr. And Mrs. Wilberforce. Henry made the introductions, and the gentlemen bowed as the ladies nodded to one another. Edward moved boldly to kiss his cousins and Fanny on both cheeks, while Mr. Wilberforce helped his wife with her wrap. She was certainly a beauty, with her long hair curling over one shoulder and her richly embroidered dark green taffeta dress revealing a slim waistline. She smiled warmly and immediately engaged the Austen ladies and Fanny in easy conversation, while the men formed a group of their own on the other side of the room. They liked Mrs. Wilberforce and felt comfortable with her immediately, getting the evening off to an encouraging start. Madame

Bigeon and her daughter attended them all with French wine and *canapes*, as the ladies settled close to the fireplace.

"Are we all here, Henry?" Jane enquired during a slight lull in the conversation.

"Not quite, Jane; I have a little surprise for you. We needed someone to balance the numbers, so we invited a gentleman whom you know fairly well," he responded. She frowned momentarily, for she never knew what to expect from Henry, but decided she could probably trust his judgement. It piqued her curiosity, though, and she was a little anxious to know who would be completing their number.

She did not have long to wait, for the sounds of a carriage were heard shortly thereafter, and Henry ushered in the Rev. James Stanier Clarke to the gathered guests. Jane could not believe her eyes and shot Henry a look that spoke volumes, but he avoided it adroitly as he carried out the introductions, deliberately coming to her last.

As Rev. Clarke approached Jane, he gave her an exaggerated courtly bow, commenting in ringing tones, "My dear Miss Jane Austen, how delighted I am to see you again and to have the opportunity to meet your lovely sister and charming young niece. I am certainly looking forward to conversing with you all this evening," he concluded grandly.

Jane did her best not to blush, not succeeding entirely in the endeavour, and tried to turn the conversation in another direction: "Why, I'm sure we're all delighted to have Mr. and Mrs. Wilberforce with us, and I know they will provide lively conversation for us all to enjoy."

William Wilberforce smiled and nodded his acknowledgement, and as Madame Bigeon opened the doors to the Dining Room to indicate that dinner was ready, Henry led them all to their places at the beautifully appointed table. After they had seated the ladies, Henry took his place at one end of the table, while Edward Cooper sat at the opposite end. Mr. Wilberforce was in the middle of the table on one side, with his wife and Fanny beside him, and Rev. Clarke was in the middle on the other side, with Cassandra closest to her cousin and Jane nearest to Henry.

When they were seated, and the conversation had begun to flow, Jane lightly kicked Henry's ankle under the table, and asked in a muted, almost strangled, voice, "Why on earth did you invite Mr. Clarke, Henry? Are you trying to make me totally miserable this evening?"

"On the contrary, my dear sister," he replied, matching her voice level, "I have great hopes that the conversation around this dinner table will be as stimulating as any you have ever experienced!" She shot him a wry look, but decided not to press the point further. Rev. Clarke was carrying on a conversation with Cassandra at the moment, and she was left to gather her wits. It wasn't long before she needed them to parry with the four diverse and very witty gentlemen gathered around Henry's table.

"Jane, I understand you've been to the Prince Regent's palace in London recently," began Edward Cooper.

Before she could answer, Rev. Clarke leaped into the conversation and responded, "As a matter of fact, I had the honour of delivering that invitation to your cousin and the delightful opportunity of conducting her around the apartments myself—on behalf of His Royal Highness, you understand," he finished elegantly. I believe that Mr. Wilberforce was having an audience with the Prince Regent about the same time."

"Ah, so you were the distinguished guest visiting Carlton House when I was there, Miss Austen," responded Wilberforce. The Prince Regent told me a famous authoress was visiting at the time, but for some reason wouldn't divulge her name. I thought it might be Fanny Burney, Madame d'Arblay, who is so popular at King George III's court. But now the mystery is cleared up."

Jane blushed in spite of the rigid control she was trying to exert, and replied, giving her brother a significant look, "Yes, if Henry had been a little more discreet, I could have continued as an unknown authoress and not had to face such scrutiny."

"But why would you not want to be known as an authoress, Miss Austen?" queried Mrs. Wilberforce. Our dear friend, Hannah More, is extremely successful in that regard. Her *Coelebs in Search of a Wife* was so popular it went into twelve editions in the first year of publication. Her success has opened up wonderful opportunities for her to speak on behalf of important causes in our country."

"I enjoyed reading that book and have urged my sister to read it as well," interrupted Cassandra. "Fanny, I think it is one that would be helpful for you at your age, with all the suitors you are attracting," she said, smiling warmly at her niece. Fanny blushed prettily but hesitated to jump into the conversation.

"I prefer to have a more quiet moral influence on the nation," Jane replied pointedly, looking around at them all.

"And so you are, Miss Austen," replied Wilberforce, "for I think your latest heroine, Fanny, in *Mansfield Park*, is very pious and indeed a paragon of virtue in the literature of our day. I commend you for creating such a thoroughly delightful creature. I believe she is my favourite of all your heroines," he concluded graciously.

"Well, thank you, sir. I appreciate the compliment, Jane responded. "I hope that all my novels will have a moral impact on the people who read them. I firmly believe we all can blend the secular and sacred in our life and work, as you have done so ably, Mr. Wilberforce."

"Indeed, I believe that is true. I have often said that God Almighty set before me two great objects: the suppression of the slave trade and the reformation of manners, he replied."

"And you have been most successful in both, my good friend," interjected Henry, smiling warmly.

"Indeed you have, Mr. Wilberforce," chimed in Mr. Clarke, "for the Duke of Clarence was just telling me the other day that he thought you the wittiest man in all of England and certainly in Parliament. He described you as being charming, an excellent mimic, and a man with a mesmerizing speaking voice."

"Well, I wish he had been that complimentary when we were in Parliament, and I was trying to persuade the Whigs and the Tories to abolish the slave trade! We had to go to some great extremes to get that result."

"In politics that may be thought necessary, but in matters of religion, I believe we should avoid extremes," Jane countered. I admit I draw characters that are a little outrageous, like Mary Bennet in *Pride and Prejudice* and Mary Crawford in *Mansfield Park*, but only to emphasize the importance of moderation in all things. I believe we should use our gifts to quietly persuade people in the right direction," she concluded.

"Oh, ho, ho," interjected Edward Cooper, "I suppose those of us who are a little more enthusiastic about it are not persuading people in a proper manner, is that it, Jane?"

"As you well know, I do find the Evangelicals too loud and noisy," Edward, and I think you must be their most boisterous cheerleader!" she parried, as much annoyed at his loudness as his boldness on the subject.

Henry touched her ankle lightly under the table at this little outburst as he jumped quickly into the conversation, "Jane, you must realise that you are surrounded by a majority of Evangelicals around this table—Mr. and Mrs. Wilberforce, Edward, and myself. And, if I'm not mistaken, your sister is leaning in that direction, if she is recommending *Coelebs in Search of a Wife*. That leaves only Fanny and Mr. Clarke to support your point of view," he concluded, eyes twinkling as usual.

"I always rise to the occasion and refuse to be intimidated when others would try to frighten me," replied Jane, rather impudently.

Cassandra interrupted long enough to say, "Why, Jane, you sound just like Lizzy in *Pride and Prejudice*," which elicited laughter from everyone around the table.

Fanny finally found her voice, and blurted, "Well, I'm currently being courted by an Evangelical clergyman, and I'm considering marrying him"—an astonishing outburst which momentarily astounded them all!

Before anyone could comment, and thinking he was coming to Jane's rescue, Rev. Clarke stated in his most indignant tone, "My dear Miss Knight, I would not recommend that course in the least!. The Evangelicals are replete with nothing but bombast and ballyhoo, and I personally will have nothing to do with their cause! And I may add that His Royal Highness, the Prince Regent, agrees entirely with me on that subject," he finished grandly.

"Well, I'm sure that you and the Prince Regent have a lot of company in that regard," replied Mr. Wilberforce mildly, "but there *is* a strong Evangelical movement afoot in this country as well as in North America that has its roots in the ministries of George Whitfield and John and Charles Wesley. And, may I say, I believe the changes in the hearts of men that their labour produced is what has saved us from the bloody revolution of our neighbours on the Continent!"

"Poppycock!" responded Mr. Clarke vehemently. "The Methodists are always overdoing things, and are so otherworldly that I find them generally embarrassing and totally out of step with the age in which we live. They are just like the Evangelicals, always carrying things a bit too far!"

Mrs. Wilberforce, animated by the discussion, leaped to her husband's defence, "When Mr. Wilberforce was first voted into Parliament as a young man, there were only two Evangelicals in that Body. And when he finally retired, there were over one hundred! And look at the good they have done in persuading Parliament to abolish the slave trade. And they have set up no less than sixty-five different societies to deal with situations as diverse as the care of animals and foreign missions. Is that not an influence of the most positive kind?"

Jane, chagrined that she might have stirred up a hornet's nest by her unguarded comment to her cousin, made an effort to pour oil on troubled waters: "I have no desire to disparage the Evangelicals to such a degree, for I do agree that Christians should be up and doing in the world."

Mr. Wilberforce smiled at her and replied, "My close friend, our former Prime Minister, William Pitt, once said to me, 'Surely the principles as well as the practice of Christianity are simple, and lead not to meditation only but to action,' and I confess I concur with his opinion."

"Yes," responded Jane, "the action of the Evangelicals and others in the abolition of the slave trade is a remarkable achievement, for which they deserve our profound gratitude. You may recall that Fanny in *Mansfield Park* raised the question of the slave trade, but was met with dead silence. So I do commend their great contribution in that regard."

"Well, I am pleased to be able to inform you that our good friend, Hannah More considers *Mansfield Park* an Evangelical novel and dear Fanny Price the epitome of the Evangelical heroine!" interjected Mrs. Wilberforce, delighted to be delivering such news.

Her husband, seeking to bolster her argument, suggested, "I know you think we Evangelicals are all addicted to raptures and bursts of delight, Miss Austen, but our happiness is often of a quiet, deep, heart-swelling sort when we feel most strongly — much like your Fanny in that particularly fine novel."

Jane relaxed a little and smiled at him and had to admit to herself that he was certainly one of the most persuasive men she had ever met!

"What is it that you most object to in the Evangelicals?" interjected Cassandra quietly. Jane was a little surprised at this comment, but then realised that her sister was trying to give her the opportunity to elaborate on her opposition to the movement, which they had discussed together a number of times in the past.

Henry entered the fray at that moment, wanting to give her a little time to formulate her opinion on the matter, "I think it has to do with the means of persuasion that Evangelicals use, does it not, Jane? he queried.

"Yes, I find too much enthusiasm quite offensive," she replied. "In fact, my next novel is going to deal with the topic of persuasion. I may even call it by that title. The heroine is persuaded by a friend of the family to reject a young Navy Captain because he does not have the means to support her in style, and goes through a long period of anxiety and depression before the situation is resolved satisfactorily. I believe we have to be very careful as to how we persuade people," she finished, seriously.

"Oh, I can't wait to read it, Aunt Jane! When will you have it finished?" exclaimed Fanny

Jane smiled indulgently at her enthusiasm, "Not for a while, Fanny. I am still working on it," she replied. "It is a difficult topic on which to achieve balance."

Mr. Wilberforce looked at her earnestly and remarked, "Indeed, it is, Miss Austen. Dr. Johnson, a man we both respect highly—if I remember our conversations in Bath correctly—had trouble achieving it, too. He commented that persuasion seems applicable to the passions, and argument to the reason, but that this distinction is not always observed. His discriminations indicated that to be persuaded may be a rational motion. So, you see, if the great man himself had difficulty in defining it, where does that leave the rest of us?" he concluded, raising his hands in a helpless gesture.

Jane was silent for a moment, deep in thought, and not having a ready answer.

"Well, I shall certainly look forward to reading your next novel to see how you have resolved that question," commented Mrs. Wilberforce, smiling. "I personally think the writer of a novel is a great persuader!" she stated enthusiastically.

"And, indeed, Miss Austen, the pen is more powerful than the sword!" remarked Mr. Wilberforce.

"I think it's the enthusiasm of the Evangelicals that offends you, cousin," said Edward, eager to keep things stirred up.

Jane glanced in his direction, and began, "It is not just your noise and bluster I dislike, although that *is* obnoxious. I find Evangelicals in the pulpit a little too eager sometimes in their delivery. However, I *could* forgive that if it came from the heart," she added.

"My dear Madam, I don't believe we can say the heart has anything to do with the delivery of a sermon! In fact, the least amount of emotion would be much preferred," interjected Mr. Clarke pompously.

"Well, I must disagree with you there," replied Henry, sparing Jane the effort, "for I believe that both reason and feeling must be applied to in dealing with divine truth, and so divine truth must be *conveyed* with both reason and feeling."

Mr. Wilberforce nodded his head vigorously and said, "I could not agree with you more, Henry. From hard experience I know that by regulating external conduct we do not change the hearts of men—and that is where the change must take place. And so, as the apostle Paul writes, 'We must persuade men.'"

"I think I must agree with that myself," mused Jane, "for I believe I put words into the mouth of Edmund Bertram, in *Mansfield Park*, to the effect that distinctness and energy may have weight in recommending the most solid truths."

"Well, then, that equates to enthusiasm in my estimation!" retorted Edward Cooper triumphantly.

Henry's eyes twinkled, and he smiled mischievously at his sister, "I think he has a good point there, Jane."

"Personally, Edward, I don't like your sermons, which are far too full of regeneration and conversion,"said Jane. "Nor do I like your letters of cruel comfort to the bereaved. And you have far too much zeal for the Bible Society," she added, a little too warmly. Edward Cooper could certainly inspire her to passionate argument whenever she was in the same room with him!

"Now, Miss Austen, I must accept some responsibility for Edward's enthusiasm, for I founded the British and Foreign Bible Society and have encouraged him to be actively involved in it," soothed Mr. Wilberforce in those dulcet tones of his. "In fact, we just had a meeting about that yesterday."

His wife responded blithely, I find the characters in your novels very much concerned with regeneration and conversion, Miss Austen, and that's one of the reasons I like them so well. I believe your Tom Bertram, in *Mansfield Park*, learned through his sufferings to repent and be forgiven. And Marianne, in *Sense and Sensibility*, needed to have time for atonement to God. So I really don't think you are far from us in that regard," she concluded sweetly.

"Well, I may say that Evangelicalism has perhaps influenced me (here she looked, pointedly, at Henry), but it hasn't yet recruited me to its ranks. I think at the moment I favour the safe, middle course between rationalism and enthusiasm and prefer to put the emphasis on personal piety," Jane countered, struggling to settle her own mind on the matter.

"If that means loving God with all your heart, soul, mind, and strength, and your neighbour as yourself," I believe our Lord would commend that," concluded Mr. Wilberforce.

That was the end of the conversation around the table, for with dinner finished, Henry rose and suggested they all adjourn to the Drawing Room to enjoy some entertainment from this accomplished group of people. With a great deal of chatter, they did so, seating themselves comfortably around the room and commenting on the gleaming pianoforte.

"Who will do the honours first?" smiled Henry, looking significantly around at the ladies of the party. "Fanny, since you are the youngest in the group, would you favour us with a song or two?" he asked.

Fanny willingly rose from her place and proceeded to the instrument, seating herself comfortably on the bench before beginning a delightful Italian aria she had been practising. She played and sang beautifully and received an enthusiastic ovation from the assembled guests. They prevailed upon her for two more and were well rewarded for their labours, for Fanny was an accomplished young lady and pleased to exhibit her talents.

Not so her Aunt Jane, for she vigorously rejected her brother's attempts to persuade her to play or sing for the assembled group, feeling her talents in that area far inferior to others in the room.

"Mrs. Wilberforce, I know you are very accomplished in both playing and singing. Would you do us the favour?" bowed Henry graciously.

"Well if you insist, I will play," she responded, moving toward the instrument, "but my husband sings so well that I will defer to him to do us the honour of singing." She looked at him with genuine affection, and he was easily persuaded to join her. Without a moment's hesitation, she began to play, and he to sing, the song that would always be his favourite:

Amazing grace! how sweet the sound
  That saved a wretch like me!
I once was lost, but now am found;
  Was blind, but now I see.

'Twas grace that taught my heart to fear,
  And grace my fears relieved;
How precious did that grace appear
  The hour I first believed!

Through many dangers, toils and snares,
  I have already come;
'Tis grace hath brought me safe thus far,
  And grace will lead me home.

When we've been there ten thousand years,
  Bright, shining as the sun,
We've no less days to sing God's praise
  Than when we'd first begun.

The Evangelicals in the room applauded enthusiastically when he was finished, while at least a couple in the group were a little less ardent in their approbation.

"You don't care much for that song, cousin?" inquired Edward Cooper mischievously. "Nor do you, Mr. Clarke?" he continued, delighted to persist in making his point.

"I don't care for the word 'wretch,'" replied Rev. Clarke vehemently. "And I might add that the Prince Regent finds it revolting as well!"

"But, my dear sir, if you believe in the doctrine of original sin, you would have to agree that we are all wretches in need of salvation," replied Mr. Wilberforce in a surprised tone.

"Yes...well...but the Liturgy is much more dignified in its approach and not as vulgar as these little ditties that are proliferating across our nation. There's far too much emphasis upon self in them and not enough upon the triune God," was Rev. Clarke's indignant reply.

"Well, then, let me sing you a song that deals with that difficulty," said Mr. Wilberforce, bowing. his head graciously. "Edward, would you accompany me on the hymn you recently composed for your churches at Yoxall and Hamstall-Ridware?"

Mrs. Wilberforce relinquished her place at the pianoforte to Edward, who played a short introduction before the rich tones of Mr. Wilberforce again rang throughout the room:

Father of heaven, whose love profound
A ransom for our souls hath found,
Before Thy throne we sinners bend,
To us thy pardoning love extend.

Almighty Son, Incarnate Word,
Our Prophet, Priest, Redeemer, Lord,
Before Thy throne we sinners bend,
To us Thy saving grace extend.

Eternal Spirit, by whose breath
The soul is raised from sin and death,
Before Thy throne we sinners bend,
To us thy quickening power extend.

Thrice holy! Father, Spirit, Son;
Mysterious Godhead, Three in One;
Before Thy throne we sinners bend,
Grace, pardon, life to us extend.

There was a pregnant pause before the warm applause began. So powerful were the words and so sweet was the singing that the audience seemed momentarily spellbound.

Henry was the first to speak: "Edward, that is profound. Indeed, I would say, it is inspired. Such an erudite trinitarian hymn deserves to be adopted by the Church of England. I hope you'll compose many more like that during your lifetime."

"I agree with you wholeheartedly," commented Mr. Wilberforce. It's becoming a favourite of mine, after *Amazing Grace*, you understand. "Is that a little more to your liking, Miss Austen?" he inquired in Jane's direction.

"Why, I suppose it cannot be faulted theologically," she replied, "although I might protest that it does have an overemphasis on pardon."

"But, Jane," began Edward, "I confess it was your written prayers that were an inspiration for me in composing that hymn. The words 'Father of heaven,' and the repetition of 'pardon' came directly from them. Your irrepressible brother, Henry, is responsible for showing the prayers to me, of course," he grinned wickedly.

"Henry, how could you?" she began and then realised it was becoming a constant refrain, and involuntarily smiled at her brother.

"Oh, what a Henry!" she said resignedly, precipitating much laughter around the room.

At that point in the proceedings, several in the party remarked that it was getting late, and they must be heading homeward. There was much chatter as everyone commented on what an enjoyable and stimulating evening it had been.

The Reverend Clarke made a particular point of conversing with Jane as the guests were departing, speaking with her in a lowered voice, "I hope, my dear Miss Austen, that my vehemence in putting forth my opinions this evening was not offensive to you. I felt I could not expostulate strongly enough on the Evangelical issue, which I myself find quite odious. However, I do think your brother's opinion on engaging the reason and emotions is worth some consideration."

"I agree it was an interesting group with some strong opinions, Mr. Clarke. But certainly the conversation was very stimulating?" queried Jane. "My brother's dinner parties are always like that."

"Well, I am pleased to have been a part of this one, to keep the conversation in balance, you understand. I think our minds are in agreement on a lot of matters, Miss Austen. I shall be writing you as soon as possible about some items of importance, but I want to urge you to avail yourself of my apartment in Golden Square for your writing endeavours. I am sure that you have at least another half dozen novels in that marvellous mind of yours," he remarked in a confidential tone." Thankfully, the other guests had left, and he had no choice but to bid her *adieu* and settle into his carriage for the trip back to Carlton House.

After everyone had left, Henry and his sisters and niece lingered longer in the Drawing Room, carrying on easy conversation as they settled into the comfortable cushions. "Well, Fanny, you certainly gave us a great surprise this evening," remarked Jane. "Why haven't we heard of this young Evangelical suitor before?" she questioned.

"Well, he's just the latest beau on my horizon," replied Fanny, impishly. "I will have to tell you all about him in the morning, for I'm much too tired to discuss the subject with you now," she yawned.

"I expect that the conversation around the breakfast table will be as stimulating as the discussion was this evening around the dinner table" commented Henry. "But, remember, your father is coming for you in the forenoon, so you and your Aunt Jane may have to continue it in your voluminous correspondence," he smiled.

"Well, I love getting letters from Aunt Jane and Aunt Cassandra, too. So perhaps we shall have to spread out the joy for as long as we can," she responded, rising from her chair. "I'm going to bed with visions of sugarplums dancing in my head!" was her last comment before disappearing up the stairs.

"I cannot believe she would consider marrying an Evangelical," mused Jane.

"And what's wrong with Evangelicals, my dear sister?" queried Henry, his mouth twitching. "I'm one, you know, and I'm your favourite brother, am I not? Would not someone like your brother Henry make her a good husband?" he prodded.

Cassandra decided to cut off the conversation at that point, replying, "Would that they were all like you, Henry!" and, taking Jane by the elbow, said, "Let us retire before we get embroiled in another discussion on Evangelicals!"

Jane lay awake for some hours in her darkened room before she could settle her mind into a mode of relaxation, allowing her to sleep. The evening's discussion had given her much to ponder. And so the authoress of four successful romantic novels, with another in process, discovered that she had a great deal to consider carefully before she could advise Fanny about what she ought to do regarding her current romantic dilemma!

Chapter 8

A Letter to Fanny Knight

23 Hans Place, London

My dearest Fanny,

I regret that we did not have more time to discuss thoroughly your dilemma regarding your Evangelical suitor. Your father came to take you back to Godmersham before we really had a chance to do more than skim the surface of the topic. It was entirely my fault for not rising earlier, but I felt quite fatigued after our exciting dinner party the evening before. I am glad you enjoyed yourself in the distinguished company Henry had invited. I know you are usually at your ease in elegant society, but it must have been something of a change for you to be having dinner with a former Member of Parliament as famous as Mr. Wilberforce, as well as a Court Chaplain and Librarian. Your Uncle Henry excels in gathering together fascinating people!

What did you think of The Reverend James Stanier Clarke? I find him quite pompous and very opinionated myself, and he certainly demonstrated that by his comments at the dinner table. He reminds me so much of Mr. Collins, in *Pride and Prejudice*. It is a wonder to me that you were able to keep your countenance when he was so indignantly outspoken about your marrying an Evangelical. As if he could judge the gentleman without ever meeting him!

But, Fanny, I must confess your announcement was something of a surprise to your Aunt Cassandra and me, as well as to your Uncle Henry. You certainly lead a much more exciting life than your aunts do, with suitors coming from all directions. Of course, that is not surprising, for you really are a lovely and accomplished young lady! How we will ever protect you from the multitude of young men wanting your attentions, I do not know. But I am sure your dear papa will be scrutinising them all very carefully! Have you asked his opinion on the matter, and what does he recommend? Oh, I know that men are not generally very intuitive about these things, but your papa is a very practical person and it would be beneficial to know how he feels about him.

I know him only through your brief description, so it is difficult for me to offer you any advice regarding him personally. As to his being an Evangelical, after our dinner discussion the other night, I am by no means convinced that we ought not all to be Evangelicals and am at least persuaded that they who are so from Reason and Feeling, must be happiest and safest. I have great respect for your Uncle Henry's opinions on the matter, and I must admit that his comments on engaging the mind and heart are very persuasive.

As to Evangelicals being unsophisticated and unacceptable in fashionable society, as you stated at breakfast the morning after the dinner, I must beg to disagree. Take, for example, the group who were gathered at Uncle Henry's little dinner party. Can you consider Mr. and Mrs. Wilberforce and even your Uncle Henry "unsophisticated" and "unacceptable in fashionable society"? I think not! But perhaps each should be accepted on his or her own personal merits.

I will grant that perhaps our cousin Edward Cooper is a little too bombastic for our taste, but it cannot be denied that he travels in sophisticated circles. He is a great friend of Mr. Wilberforce and of The Reverend Thomas Gisborne, of Yoxall Lodge, who were at Cambridge together. So they are all very much at ease with one another. Your Aunt Cassandra highly recommends Mr. Gisborne's book, *An Enquiry into the Duties of the Female Sex*, which I think you ought to read. I had quite determined not to read it, but after she persuaded me, I told her tht I was pleased with it and glad that she had recommended it.

I am indeed sorry that I cannot offer you any more explicit advice than this. Perhaps if you could persuade the young man to come to London when I am here, or to visit Chawton, your Aunt Cassandra and I might be able to take his measure and see if he is worthy of you. In the meantime, take care, and do not let your heart be too easily won!

I am always affectionately,
your own Aunt Jane

Chapter 9

A Christmas Gathering

A few days after the dinner party, Henry arranged to convey his sisters back to Chawton in his barouche. Jane seemed a little sluggish in recovering from that late night, and Cassandra was concerned enough to draw it to Henry's attention. "She is not as energetic as was her wont," she commented.

Henry had to agree, "I've noticed since my illness that she doesn't have the stamina she had before," he replied. "Perhaps getting her back home to familiar surroundings will help her," he concluded.

Jane was very happy to comply, as the hustle and bustle of London had begun to wear on her, and she was not as anxious to go out and about as she had been.

The Summer months at Chawton, usually so welcome, had weeks that were hot and uncomfortable for everyone, but especially Jane. The pain in her back increased, and she began to have little fainting spells, to the point that Cassandra finally insisted that she see Dr. Lyford. Jane was reluctant, but realised that she herself needed to know the source of her physical distress. Dr. Lyford did what he could to make her situation more comfortable, but suggested that she should perhaps visit the spa at Cheltenham or Bath to see if the waters might help her.

Accordingly, as Autumn set in, Cassandra and Jane packed their clothes and Jane's manuscripts for the journey to Cheltenham in Gloucestershire. They had written to The Reverend Fowle, family friend and father of Cassandra's deceased *fiance*, to see if they might break their journey with him. He had replied, assuring them of a warm welcome. And so the two sisters set out in Edward's carriage (he was at the Great House in Chawton at this time) to their first destination. On their arrival the Fowles immediately set about making Jane as comfortable as possible in their charming rectory. Cassandra and Mrs. Fowle talked of books they had read recently, and the conversation turned to Hannah More and *Coelebs in Search of a Wife*. "Jane, have you read her excellent book?" questioned Mrs. Fowle.

"Cassandra has been pressing it on me, but I confess that she has by no means raised my curiosity about it," she replied. "I admit that my disinclination for it before was affected, but now it is real, for I do not like the Evangelicals."

"Well, if that is the case, I can understand why you would not want to read it, but really, my dear, it is one of the best books I have read," exclaimed Mrs. Fowle. "I will be happy to lend you my copy for your journey to Cheltenham," she offered, graciously.

"Thank you; that is very kind," replied Jane. "Of course I shall be delighted when I read it, like other people, but until I do, I dislike it."

"Well, we will see how you feel about it when you return from Cheltenham," she soothed.

Two days later Cassandra and Jane continued their journey to the spa city, travelling in Mr. Fowle's coach, mercifully lent to them by their affable host. The Fowles and Austens had been friends for many years, and Jane's father had taught the Fowle sons at Steventon rectory when they were young boys. That is how Cassandra had met and fallen in love with their dear, departed son.

The sisters settled in to rented accommodation for a month at Cheltenham, hoping that taking the waters would relieve whatever was ailing Jane and restore her to health again. But as the weeks went by, she seemed no better, and sometimes even worse. To while away the time, Jane read Hannah More's book and had to admit that it was well worth reading by any young lady in search of a suitable husband. But she was far beyond that at this point, and certainly couldn't recommend herself to any gentleman with her current health in such a precarious situation. She had to admit than even her complexion was being adversely affected.

At the end of the month's stay Cassandra was very glad to be returning to Chawton via Kintbury, to get her sister back under Dr. Lyford's care. The journey was long, but thankfully broken at the Fowle rectory, where they were received just as graciously as before. Jane was happy to report that she had enjoyed the book and thanked Mrs. Fowle for recommending it and loaning it to her. Soon they were back in her beloved Hampshire, able to relax in familiar surroundings under the consummate care of Martha Lloyd. The three chairs were put together in the Living Room for Jane to rest, as her mother continued to occupy the sofa at some point almost every day. Jane made visits to Dr. Lyford in Alton whenever the pain or debilitating weakness became too much for her, until eventually the doctor had to make the trip to visit her.

As Christmas drew near, Frank and his family came and settled in at the Great House in Chawton, which had been rented to him by his brother, Edward. He immediately set out for the cottage to spend time with his mother and sisters, for he had been away at sea for far too long. Jane welcomed this very practical brother of hers, for she had not spent much time with him since they had lived together with him and his wife, Mary, in Southampton. There she had seen his ability to make a house a home, using his excellent carpentry skills to make the place more comfortable. Frank had read all of her novels, which were posted to him at the closest port, and was justly proud of his accomplished authoress sister.

Frank was not very tall and at times could be rather brusque—probably quite essential in his position in the Navy. She knew he would certainly be promoted to Admiral at some point in his career, for he displayed all the qualities necessary for that exalted position. As a young boy his family members had called him "Fly," for he loved to fly over the hills on a little pony he had purchased with his own money. And, with his pragmatic bent, Frank, had eventually sold the animal for a profit. His family had grown in size and were all ensconced at this time in the Great House, which was large enough to accommodate them.

As Cassandra watched Jane's health deteriorate to the point where she needed a donkey cart to ride to Alton, an idea took shape in her mind to gather the whole Austen family together at Christmas. With the Napoleonic wars settled, both naval brothers were on leave at the same time, which was very unusual. Edward was applied to for the use of the Great House for a Christmas feast and was happy to comply with his favourite sister's request. He and his family would come from Godmersham for the festive occasion, and join the others in Chawton. Charles would do the same from London, with his three girls. Henry would bring them himself and make sure he was there for the festivities. James and his family could easily come the short distance from Steventon. So, it was all arranged, but kept a secret from Jane, for Cassandra wanted it to be a surprise for her beloved sister.

She and Martha Lloyd made most of the preparations, deciding that all the children could be served an hour before the adults sat down to dinner. Edward's cooks and serving staff were happy to do their part to make this a delightful occasion for the Austen and Knight families. The older cousins could look after the younger ones and entertain them in one of the large rooms upstairs in the Great House, while the elders ate together. They would provide enough games to keep the little ones busy. The decorations were arranged in every room, with large wreaths throughout, and garlands of holly and ivy on the banisters of the great staircase and on every fireplace mantlepiece. Plenty of wood was cut and piled to keep the fires roaring against the chill of Winter. The place had never looked so lively and festive!

None of these preparations were permitted to involve Jane, who assumed that there would be the usual small gathering at the cottage. They enjoyed the traditional candlelight service at St. Nicholas Church, but this time Frank read the Christmas lesson from Matthew's account. This was her brother who was known as the Navy Officer who knelt in church. She could tell his whole heart was in the reading and was proud to notice that the rough life in the Navy had not diminished his reverence for things sacred. Their father had written him a long letter when he was preparing to go to the Naval College at Porstmouth at the age of 12, which she knew he had kept close to his heart all these years. She could see that he had kept to the principles his father had reminded him about at that time.

The next day, Henry arrived at the cottage in his carriage, having left Charles and his children at the Great House. Jane and her mother were wrapped up against the cold and transported there, just a short distance away. Jane was delighted to see Henry and couldn't wait to sit down with him for a long conversation. That was not to be, for when she arrived at the Great House, she could not believe her eyes. Nephews and nieces, old and young, surrounded her and welcomed her with a clamour she could not believe! She was amazed to see all of her siblings there, except poor George, but she knew his brothers would make a point of visiting him later in the day and taking him some special Christmas savoury treats. That was one of the tender traditions of the Austen family.

They placed Jane on the sofa nearest to the fireplace in the Great Room, with Henry and Cassandra beside her, and her other brothers gathered around her in comfortable chairs. Her mother sat on the other side of the fireplace, with James close beside her. Martha and the two Marys, James' and Frank's wives, were in the Dining Room supervising the first sitting, which consisted of all the Austen and Knight children. As large as the room was, it was difficult to accommodate everyone, and they had to add smaller tables around the periphery of the room. Charles' daughters were a little shy at first, since they had not seen their cousins very often, but the older ones pampered and teased them gently, and soon they felt at home. It was amazing to see all eleven of Edward's children getting along so well with all of Frank's, for they were the two largest groups seated at the tables. There was plenty of noise, but generally they were well behaved, under the watchful eye of the Marys and the indefatigable and unflustered Martha.

In the Great Room, Jane looked around at her family members and marvelled that they were all together at last. She had written, in *Mansfield Park*, and it was certainly *appropos* for this occasion:

Children of the same family, the same blood, with the same first associations and habits, have some means of enjoyment in their power which no subsequent connections can supply; and it must be by a long and unnatural estrangement, by a divorce which no subsequent connection can justify, if such precious remains of the earliest attachments are ever entirely outlived.

It had been many years since every one of them had been in the same room at the same time. It lacked only her father and George to being the complete family circle. "I cannot believe that you have all come to celebrate Christmas together with me!" she exclaimed.

"We would not have missed it for the world, Jane," replied Frank. "It is far too long since we have been together like this." Then they all chimed in together in the same vein, talking over one another, and finally breaking up in laughter because no one voice could be heard distinctly above the clamour.

"Do you remember our Christmas plays in the barn, when one of us would write the drama, and another would write the prologue, and we would all act our parts for the assembled family and guests?" asked Jane, eyes shining. "Oh, those were such wonderful times, and they are such pleasant memories," she concluded, sighing. Again there was the hubbub of sound as they all jumped in, trying to make their voices heard. And once more they broke up in laughter that they all were still so competitive.

Martha Lloyd looked in at the doorway, wondering what all the commotion was about. Cassandra turned quickly in her direction, and inquired, "Is everything well with the children?" She nodded affirmatively and closed the door quietly. It did her heart good to see them enjoying each other as they celebrated their talented sister.

Soon it was the turn of the adults to move to the Dining Room for their Christmas dinner together. There was turkey, as well as goose and ham, with all the trimmings, set before them on a beautifully decorated table. There was no sign of any of the children, for they had all been ushered to the upper floors to play games and be entertained by the older ones. There was a moment of hesitation while it was determined who should give thanks for the bountiful meal, but they all deferred to James (and his mother insisted), that he say grace:

"Gracious Father, Lord of Heaven and Earth, we give Thee heartfelt thanks for the plenty with which Thou hast blessed this table at this joyous season of the year, when we celebrate the birth of Thy Son, our Saviour. We are most thankful for Thy mercy and grace in bringing us together for this happy reunion of our widespread families. And we are particularly grateful for Thy bringing into the world our celebrated sister, Jane. We thank Thee for the gifts Thou hast bestowed upon her and pray that Thou would'st restore her to health and strength and allow her sweet presence to be amongst us for many years to come. In the name of our gracious Saviour, (and they all uttered a heartfelt) Amen!"

The men fell to the feast before them with hearty appetites, while the three ladies ate much more daintily. Jane's appetite returned for the occasion, and she ate better than she had for many a month. They all rejoiced to see the light in her eyes, even though her cheeks had lost their accustomed rosy glow. There was plenty of light banter and teasing, as one after another recalled joyful times in the rectory at Steventon. James remembered the creaking weathervane that bothered one of the schoolboy boarders their father was tutoring, as the young lad tried to get to sleep in the attic. Their mother recalled the poem she had written about it.

Cassandra mentioned the time her brothers and young Tom Fowle bounded down the stairs, hallooing about something and racing out of the back door into the green field beyond to roll down the grassy slope. Charles remembered the times when he had to catch the stagecoach for Portsmouth at the Deane Gate Inn, when he was enrolled at the Naval College. He was pleased and proud to be following in his brother Frank's footsteps, but it was so difficult to leave his beloved family behind. Edward talked about the day he departed Steventon to be adopted into Thomas Knight's family, and how strange it felt to be leaving behind the boisterous rectory for the solitary, childless mansion at Godmersham. Had the Knights not been so kind and nurturing, he said he would have felt very homesick indeed.

Frank chimed in his recollection about the awful Winter when the basement had flooded, and the odour of dampness had clung to the place until the doors could be open all day and the place aired out. They all remembered that time and wrinkled their noses at the poignant memory. Henry chuckled about his days at Oxford with James, when they had published *The Loiterer* anonymously and recruited Jane to write an article for it. That moved Jane to express heart-felt sentiments, her voice crackling with emotion, "And no sister has ever had dearer siblings than I have, and I am blessed to be related to you all, and on this happy occasion to be among you all!"

The plum pudding had been consumed by then, and there were a few misty eyes as they moved away from the table. The noise from the children upstairs was beginning to penetrate their senses, and a few of the younger ones were straggling down the staircase, trying to find their parents. Mrs. Austen asked to return to the cottage, for she was rather weary from the combination of the Christmas Eve and Christmas Day festivities. Henry handed her and Cassandra into his barouche, while James and Charles, with his girls, walked with Mary and Martha down the lane to join them at the cottage. Jane knew her brothers would take this opportunity to go and visit their brother, George.

Frank and his Mary rushed upstairs to quell some of the noise and thumping they could hear. When Edward had seated Jane comfortably on the sofa by the fire, she requested that he go upstairs and ask some of her older nieces and nephews to come and gather around her. She particularly wanted his Fanny and William, and James' three to join her. Edward was happy to comply with her request, and soon her five favourites were sitting close to her—the girls gathered on the sofa, and the boys lounging at her feet on the floor.

She looked at them all longingly and then beamed her sunny smile at them, as she spoke, somewhat haltingly, "I cannot express to you...adequately...how very...dear...you all are to me...and...how much I have enjoyed your...delightful company...through the years." They were a little awestruck at the tiredness they saw in her face and the seriousness with which she was addressing them.

But Fanny, who was almost like a sister to her, plucked up her courage and exclaimed, "Dear Aunt Jane, we love you dearly and admire you immensely, and you are indeed our *favourite* aunt!"

William, encouraged by this, reached up and patted her hand, and said, "We remember all the times you got down on the floor and played spillikins with us."

Young Caroline put her arm in Aunt Jane's, and chirped, "And all those stories you made up for us—I always thought they were real!"

Jane smiled at them all and reached out to put her hand on James Edward's curly head. He looked up at the familiar face and said, with some emotion, "Your clergymen characters in your novels have entertained me immensely, Aunt Jane, "and the reality of them—along with my father's example—has led me to consider taking Holy Orders."

"I'm going to do the same," offered William, simply.

"I could not be happier about that!" replied Jane, greatly moved by their sincerity. "And what will you girls do?" she inquired of her three nieces.

"I plan to write romantic novels just like you, Aunt Jane," vowed Anna.

"Me, too, me, too!" cried Caroline, animatedly.

Jane interrupted long enough to say, "Your Uncle Henry once told me that someone had remarked to him that my novels were much too clever to have been written by a woman." They all laughed spontaneously at that!

Fanny took her time, remarking, "I want to marry a handsome man of noble birth and have many children who will remind me of you," she finished.

Jane laughed out loud at that remark, and reached out to hug them all individually. "Those plans suit you all very well," she declared, settling back on the soft sofa cushions. "You are all greatly gifted in a number of ways, and it is important that you recognise the ways in which your Creator has endowed you, and pursue those callings in life," she stated, serious again. Our father, your dear late grandpapa, had long talks with each of your aunts and uncles and encouraged us to follow the path that the Lord had laid out for us. He urged us to pursue—in whatever we did—His honour and glory before all else," and that is what we have tried to do," she concluded.

"Well, God has certainly gifted you, Aunt Jane," replied James Edward, "for those characters that came out of your imagination certainly seem very real to all of us, and they are having a very good influence in the whole world!"

Jane beamed at him and replied, playfully, "Your Uncle Henry writes very superior sermons, James Edward. You and I must try to get hold of one or two and put them into our novels: it would be a fine help to a volume, and we could make our heroine read it aloud on a Sunday evening."

"We heard you even went to Carlton House in London, and the Prince Regent has all your novels in all his palaces, and the royal princesses are reading them!" cried Caroline.

"Yes, it is true," replied Jane, "I saw them there myself. It is a wonder to me that the Lord would allow me write novels that find their way into a prince's palaces, but so it is," she remarked, wonderingly.

"We want to be just like you, Aunt Jane, and we don't want you ever to leave us!" exclaimed Anna, with feeling. They all had glistening eyes at that point, and Caroline was starting to cry.

Jane hugged her warmly, and said, brightly, "Don't cry, Caroline. I have a delightful story about princes and princesses ready to send to you, and I will make sure you get it soon." That cheered the little girl immensely,

Jane quickly intervened to keep all their thoughts and emotions from getting out of hand: "I remember your dear grandpapa used to quote to us from *Ecclesiastes*:

There is nothing better for a man,
  than that he should eat and drink,
and that he should make his soul
  enjoy good in his labour....
To every thing there is a season,
  and a time to every purpose under the heaven;
A time to be born, and a time to die....

"Oh, don't talk about dying, Aunt Jane!" interrupted Caroline.

Jane drew her close and continued, "I thought that was rather serious at the time, but I have lived long enough to learn the truth of it. My soul—my very inward being—can experience enjoyment in my labour of writing, as long as my attitude is that it should glorify God and serve His kingdom. Oh, I hope you all experience the sheer joy that I have had in knowing that God is pleased with the labour of my hands!" she exclaimed, clasping those hands and looking around at them, lovingly.

Those were her last words to them, for the door of the room opened and Henry's face appeared. "I think it's time we took your Aunt Jane back to Chawton cottage," he said. The children rose, one by one, and gave their Uncle Henry a big hug, as he came into the room. He reached down and kissed his sister, tenderly, and then draped her in the woollen shawl he had brought in his barouche. Her five favourites wistfully waved goodbye at the front door until the carriage was completely out of sight down the long driveway.

Soon Jane was snug in the little Hampshire cottage that had become so dear to her. As she lay in bed with Cassandra, drifting slowly off to sleep after the exciting evening, she remarked to her sister, "It was such a special time with my nieces and nephews tonight, Cassandra. I felt...inspired, I think,...to urge them to follow their gifts and callings, as I and all of their aunts and uncles have been able to do. It makes me realise how wise our dear, departed papa was in recognising those in each of us, and making sure we had the equipment and training to carry them forward to completion! Do you not think so, Cassandra?" she queried.

"I do indeed, Jane. I do indeed!" she replied.

Chapter 10

A Letter to Caroline Austen

Chawton Cottage, Hampshire

My dear, sweet Caroline,

How delightful it was to spend time with you and my other nieces and nephews after our Christmas dinner with everyone at the Great House. Was it not just the best of Christmas celebrations? I was so pleased that the whole family could be together. It has been many years since that has been possible. Your Uncle Frank and Uncle Charles have been at sea so much, and it seems that the Austens and Knights are scattered all around Hampshire, Kent, and London. But this was a festive season to be remembered, and I am grateful to have had you all in one place!

Dear Caroline, I love your sweet ways and romantic notions. Have I told you lately that you remind me very much of myself as a young girl? I was always so idealistic and was often teased about having my head in the clouds. Well, if being imaginative and creative is having one's head in the clouds, then I am all for it. Without that, my dear niece, none of your Aunt Jane's novels would have been written and published.

So, I encourage you to carry on in your romantic ways and keep putting your thoughts down on paper, no matter how much others may vex you. I remember people saying I was affected and silly when I was your age, but I have not heard them saying that lately! If you will go on, just being your sweet self and thinking your happy thoughts, who knows what may come from your pen?

Whatever you create I will be most anxious to read, Caroline. So, please feel free to send your Aunt Jane anything you want her to read. And know that she stands ready to help you with any writing on any topic that might interest you.

I have been working on a "royal romance" that I thought might bring you some pleasure. I wrote it with you in mind and hope that you will enjoy it. I have left the ending unfinished so that you may complete it, if you like. Perhaps, you might be inspired to write something like it, or something very different. Pray let me know what you think about it.

Always your loving and affectionate,
Aunt Jane

In a land that was lush and green and flowing with many rivers lived a handsome king and his wife and family of many children. They had several palaces with beautiful gardens that they could enjoy all year long. The king was noble and wanted to raise his children to be kind and thoughtful and to set a good example to everyone in the realm.

Unfortunately, his oldest son, George, rebelled against his father and gathered around him a group of friends who encouraged him to do evil things. They wanted to do nothing but throw lavish parties, spend money foolishly, and be involved in vile activities. The king's son liked many women but would never settle down to marry one who would be suitable to be the next queen of the realm. Finally, his gambling debts got to be so monstrous that he had to agree to marry a princess with enough money to pay them off!

This princess, named Caroline, (just like you!) lived in another land, so the prince had to send ships to carry her to his country. One of the ships got lost in the fog and was missing for five days before it met up with the others. All the sailors laughed at those on the ship that had been lost and made them feel very foolish. At last, the princess was ready to come aboard to meet the important people the prince had sent to meet her, including his personal chaplain. She smiled and held out her hand to have it kissed by all his noble courtiers. Then they sat down to a sumptuous dinner prepared in her honour.

The chaplain conducted divine service on Sunday for those on board the ship, and the princess smiled and talked with him after it was finished. He thought she was very nice. Soon they arrived in the prince's country, where the wedding was to take place immediately. However, when the prince met the princess, he was not very happy. She was not as pretty as he thought she should be, and he really didn't want to marry her. But it was the only way to pay his debts, so he reluctantly went through with the ceremony.

About a year later they had a baby, whom they named Charlotte. Her mama and papa loved her very much and wanted to give her the best of everything. But her father did not like her mother and sent her away to another country to live. But everybody in the prince's court loved little Charlotte, and she grew up to be a lovely young lady with a sweet smile that won everybody's heart. Her father wanted her to marry a fine young prince, so he brought several from other lands to meet his daughter. Princess Charlotte fell in love with one of them and wanted to marry him.

Her father agreed and gave them a lavish wedding in his palace, with a wonderful feast, to which many nobles in the land were invited. He also built them a beautiful palace in which to live together. Princess Charlotte was delighted that she could finally have a palace of her own in which to raise a family with her handsome prince.

Chapter 11

A Final Farewell

There was great bustle in Chawton cottage, as Cassandra and Martha Lloyd scurried around, gathering and packing Jane's belongings for the journey to Winchester. Martha's sister, Mary, James' wife, had come in their carriage, and was standing silently by, ready to accompany them to help Cassandra nurse Jane. Dr. Lyford considered it best that Jane be moved to that city for closer observation and treatment. The journey might have been more pleasant had the May day not dawned cloudy and rainy. But Jane was carefully wrapped up, and James' carriage was pulled as close to the door as possible. James had not come, as he had not been feeling well for some time. Henry and Edward's William mounted their horses, determined to accompany their dear relative to 8 College Street, the house in Winchester that Jane's old friend, Elisabeth Bigg Heathcote, had rented for her. She was the widow of William Heathcote, formerly Prebendary of Winchester Cathedral, and lived nearby in the Cathedral Close. And she had nearly been Jane's sister-in-law, for it was her brother who had proposed marriage to Jane when she was much younger.

Seated in the carriage with her beloved Cassandra by her side, Jane looked out at her brother and nephew riding in the pouring rain. "No one was ever loved more dearly than I am!" she exclaimed. Mary looked at Cassandra and lifted her eyebrows, wondering what to do.

Cassandra squeezed Jane's hand and replied, warmly, "And no one was ever more worthy of it, Jane!" She put her arm around her sister, and Jane laid her head on Cassandra's shoulder.

They were all glad when the sodden journey was ended, and they were able to warm themselves by the fire that had been kindled in anticipation of their arrival. Elizabeth had thoughtfully provided refreshments for them, and they felt better as early evening set in and the rain abated.

As the men of the party prepared to mount their horses and return to Chawton, Henry remarked, "Let us hope it won't be raining like it was today when we come again to take you back home, Jane." Then they were off, and the three women were left alone to settle in to the strange, but comfortable surroundings. They talked quietly together, as Cassandra and Mary made Jane as comfortable as possible.

Winchester College was right next door, so there was much activity on the short street. The Drawing Room looked out on to a huge wall surrounding the majestic old Cathedral across the road from them. A huge gate at one end of the street led to the Cathedral Close, with its venerable old buildings. Jane had a warming sensation of feeling close to the place she had loved and revered through the years and was pleased to be able to settle down early for the night in the bed they had placed in the Living Room for her, since the journey on rutted roads in the rain had tired her.

Dr. Lyford came in the forenoon, and after examining her, seemed cautiously optimistic that she would not have to stay in Winchester for long. Mary went out to do some shopping for their needs and left the sisters to talk together in easy companionship. Although these were strange surroundings for Jane, she had Cassandra to cheer her and was thankful for such a loving and faithful sister.

Jane passed the days in letter-writing and conversation, staying mostly indoors, as she had not the strength to walk more than across the room. She had days when she felt a little better and others when she was seized with faintness. The increasing pain in her back was diminished by the laudanum that Dr. Lyford administered, but he gradually had to increase the dosage. Jane did not like the stupour that the laudanum effected, but neither did she like the pain she experienced without it. So she was having an uncomfortable struggle maintaining physical and emotional equilibrium under these trying circumstances. And she could not bear to look in a mirror at her mottled complexion and the thinness of her cheeks. Her looks had diminished considerably in the last few months! But, most of all, Jane didn't enjoy being a patient, and longed to be up and about enjoying the early Summer weather.

One weekend when she was feeling stronger, Elizabeth Heathcote came to visit for a half hour and reminisced with Jane about the balls they had attended in Basingstoke when they were much younger. The session cheered Jane immensely, and as Elizabeth departed, Cassandra followed her downstairs to the street and asked if she might come in her carriage the next morning to take Jane to the morning service at the Cathedral. Elizabeth was more than willing to be involved in such a delightful task for her old friends.

The next morning, Cassandra helped Jane into her best dress, "just to make you feel better," suggested Cassandra. After a little breakfast of toast and tea, they heard the unmistakeable sounds of a carriage pulling up below their window. In the next moment, Elisabeth was in the room, smiling, "How would you like to attend Divine Service at the Cathedral, Jane?" she asked.

Jane looked from Elizabeth to Cassandra, realising they had arranged the event to surprise her. "Oh, that would be wonderful!" she exclaimed. "I have so longed to hear again the great hymns and that wonderful organ," she finished.

They helped her down the stairs slowly and with a little difficulty, but soon she was ensconced in the comfortable carriage and being carried the short distance to the Cathedral. Jane was not able to rise for the singing of the hymns, but she sat throughout the service on a cushion Elizabeth had thoughtfully brought for her. Jane's eyes glistened with tears as the organ swelled to play, just before the sermon, a hymn by her favourite poet, William Cowper:

The Spirit breathes upon the Word,
And brings the truth to sight;
Precepts and promises afford
A sanctifying light.

A glory gilds the sacred page,
Majestic, like the sun:
It gives a light to every age;
It gives, but borrows none.

The hand that gave it still supplies
The gracious light and heat;
His truths upon the nations rise;
They rise, but never set.

Let everlasting thanks be Thine,
For such a bright display
As makes a world of darkness shine
With beams of heavenly day.

My soul rejoices to pursue
The steps of Him I love,
Till glory breaks upon my view,
In brighter worlds above.

Jane had to admit that her mind wandered during the sermon, for she was moved by the poet's sincere, heartfelt words. William Cowper had been her father's favourite as well, and he had introduced the remarkable man's works to his whole family during after-dinner readings at Steventon rectory. It was indelibly imprinted upon her mind that Cowper had suffered from deep depression and that his life had been cut short by suicide in 1800 while he was in a depressive state of mind. Jane wondered how many more beautiful poems he might have penned, had he lived longer. She pondered what the "glory" was like in "brighter worlds above." She could not help thinking that she still had more novels to write if the Lord would grant her more time. A new novel, called *Sanditon*, about a small seaside resort that was becoming popular, was her latest attempt at writing....

She was startled back to reality by the thunder of the organ, as it began the closing hymn—another one by Cowper, and her father's favourite. She could hardly believe her ears, for it was one that they had sung at her father's memorial service in Bath:

O for a closer walk with God
A calm and heavenly frame,
A light to shine upon the road
That leads me to the Lamb!

Where is the blessedness I knew
When first I saw the Lord?
Where is the soul-refreshing view
Of Jesus and His word?

What peaceful hours I once enjoyed!
How sweet their memory still!
But they have left an aching void
The world can never fill.

Return, O holy Dove! Return,
 Sweet messenger of rest!
I hate the sins that made Thee mourn,
 And drove Thee from my breast.

The dearest idol I have known
 Whate'er that idol be,
Help me to tear it from Thy throne,
 And worship only Thee.

So shall my walk be close with God,
 Calm and serene my frame;
So purer light shall mark the road
 That leads me to the Lamb.

As the sound of the organ and congregational singing faded, Jane sat with her eyes closed, tears spilling copiously down her cheeks. Cassandra knew what she was thinking and how she was feeling, for she herself had been moved at the words she had last heard at their father's service. She put her arm around her sister and handed her a lace-embroidered handkerchief she was carrying in her purse.

"I understand, Jane. It brings back painful memories," does it not?

Jane, dabbing at her tears, looked up at Cassandra and said, with a sob in her voice, "I miss our father....I want to go home now."

Late May faded into June, and June into early July, with ups and downs in the patient's condition.. The weather was hot and oppressive on some days, and Jane struggled for breath, alarming Cassandra. Dr. Lyford was summoned and advised propping the patient up on the pillows so that she could breathe more easily. He looked concerned as he drew Cassandra aside and commented, "Your sister is not improving at the rate I had expected. Her pulse and breathing this morning are quite erratic, and she is in some discomfort. I can continue the laundanum for the pain to make her more comfortable, but her condition does not look promising, Miss Austen. I wish I could offer you more hope, but I think you should be prepared for the worst. I do not believe the end is in immediate sight, but she may have more spells of faintness and weakness in the days ahead." Cassandra looked anxiously into his face and nodded numbly. The doctor waved to Mary and Jane as he left, and Cassandra rejoined them, trying to put on a cheerful face.

Jane, however, knew her sister and her own body too well and realized that her life might be coming to its end on earth. That afternoon she called Cassandra to her bedside and insisted on dictating her will to her sister, asking her to disperse carefully the few items that she held dear and the small amount of money she had been able to save from the publishing of her novels. Cassandra sat rigidly through this exercise, trying not to show emotion, but she was shaken inside when it was over. She asked Mary to send an urgent message to Henry to let him know how serious the situation had become, and suggested that Mary might want to take a rest if Henry were able to come. Mary nodded her assent and left on the errand.

The next day Henry arrived in Edward's carriage, and the two sisters were overjoyed to see him. Mary, feeling thoroughly stressed and somewhat exhausted, reluctantly bade the patient adieu. "We have not always seen eye to eye, Mary," remarked Jane, as her sister-in-law was preparing to leave, "but you have always been a good sister to me." Mary kissed her on the forehead, and was grateful for the comfortable carriage that would return her to Steventon.

"Now that you are here, Henry, you shall see vast improvement in me," exclaimed Jane, "for your cheerful temper will encourage me to be my old self again."

Henry held her hand to his lips and kissed it in his most courtly manner, proclaiming "Dr. Henry Austen at your service, Ma'am!" but inwardly he cringed at the deterioration that was very evident in her countenance. Cassandra and Henry talked long after the patient had gone to sleep that evening, discussing what they must do to prepare for the eventuality of her leaving them.

"She has made her will," said Cassandra, "but there are at least two more complete novels and part of another one not published. And I know she would want to be buried in her beloved Winchester Cathedral, if that were possible," continued Cassandra, her eyes glistening with tears.

"I know they have not buried many women there, particularly if they are not of the nobility, but let me see what James and I can do for her," responded Henry sympathetically. "Our father had strong connections with the Dean, and James and I know others there, and we can perhaps persuade them to our cause."

"That would be wonderful if you could bring that about, Henry. How blessed she is to have had such a father, and now brothers who are thus connected," she concluded, kissing him on the cheek.

The next morning Henry walked over to Winchester Cathedral to try to talk with the Dean about the possibility of his sister being buried there when the necessity should arise. He first found a particular friend of James, who went with him to present the request. He was received graciously and with some sympathy, but then had to wait all afternoon, for others had to be consulted concerning the unusual request. But when he returned to his sisters, there was a slight spring in his step, for the required permission had been granted!

Early that evening, as Jane's mind wandered in and out of consciousness, she became more alert. She smiled wanly at Henry and Cassandra sitting close by her and tried to talk, but could barely whisper, "Am I dying?" Her sister choked and could not utter a word.

Henry took Jane's hand in his, and smiled encouragingly, "Jane, only God knows. We are praying that you will recover, as I did. But if He should desire to take you to be with Him, we want you to know that Cassandra and I will make sure that your last novels are published." She tried to nod her head in understanding. "And, my dear sister, permission has been granted for you to be buried in your beloved Cathedral." A light came into her eyes then, and she lay back on the pillow, seemingly content.

The next morning, St. Swithun's Day, Jane astonished them by rallying and rousing herself, and requesting writing paper. "You see, Henry, what a tonic you are for me!" she exclaimed in a stronger voice than they had heard in some time. Then she proceeded to write, in the space of about an hour, a delightful poem about St. Swithun. Jane read it to her brother and sister, who applauded wholeheartedly the sentiments contained therein and remarked on the strength which she had received to write it. Incredulous, Cassandra and Henry looked at each other and wondered if God had granted them their earnest petitions on her behalf!

That afternoon she surprised them again by asking for more paper to write to William, Edward's son, who had confided to her at Chawton his desire to take Holy Orders and become Rector of Steventon Church. He had been so proud to be following in his grandfather's footsteps. "I feel I must write Edward," she said, and set about the task, writing slowly and carefully, with long pauses in which she pondered her words carefully. Finally, when she had finished the page, she handed it to Cassandra and asked her to seal it and send it to William as soon as she could.

Later that evening, as if exhausted by this burst of energy, she sank back in the pillows, restlessly moaning. When they enquired what she needed, she whispered hoarsely, "Pray for me, oh, pray for me." Alarmed, they summoned Dr. Lyford, who came quickly, administering a heavier dose of laudanum than usual to deaden the pain she was experiencing. He was amazed at their reports that she had rallied that morning, but gave them no more hope than he had on his last visit. "The pulse and breathing are still erratic, and that gives me unremitting cause for concern," he commented in a serious tone.

Jane sank into a deep sleep then and did not stir until well into mid-morning. Henry had stayed up with her through the night, giving Cassandra some needed rest. He had prayed for her most of that time, as she had requested, asking God to spare her to serve Him longer, "if it be Thy will," he concluded. During his vigil he realized how stressful it must have been for Jane as she sat by his bedside just eighteen months ago, pleading for his life to be spared. And God had raised him up to health and the strength he now felt. As he convalesced back then, Henry had decided to leave banking and enter the ministry of the Church, like his father and brother James. Illnesses can be life-changing experiences, he thought. Perhaps his sister would be spared, as he had been, to further God's kingdom with her writing!

The next morning, she stirred from her deep sleep of the night before, and whispered that she had dreamed about golden streets. She asked Henry to read to her about the streets of gold. Her brother had his Bible with him and turned to the final chapters of *Revelation* to read:

> *And the twelve gates were twelve pearls;*
> *every several gate was of one pearl:*
> *and the street of the city was pure gold,*
> *as it were transparent glass.*
> *And I saw no temple therein:*
> *for the Lord God Almighty and the Lamb*
> *are the temple of it.*

> *And the city had no need of the sun,*
> *neither of the moon, to shine in it:*
> *for the glory of God did lighten it,*
> *and the Lamb is the light thereof.*

Jane visibly relaxed then, and Cassandra saw the hint of a smile at the corner of her lips. She kept watch that night, as Henry took some rest. Jane was more restless at times and then became very weak and still, so that her sister bent over to listen closely to see if she was still breathing.

In the morning, the erratic breathing was still evident, and she stirred again from her listless state. Cassandra plumped Jane's pillows and tried to get some liquid past her parched lips. Henry rose after a restless night and came to Cassandra's rescue. Sister and brother exchanged meaningful glances as they watched her deteriorate even more during that day. That afternoon, they sat together by the bed, watching Jane's head moving slightly with every shallow breath. During their silent vigil, the light of the sun moved round to the place where it streamed in the bow window and fell across her bed. Jane's eyes suddenly fluttered, but didn't open. "I feel warm...I see the sun," she whispered.

"Yes, Jane, the sun is shining on you," replied Cassandra.

"I see...lots of sunbeams dancing around the bright sun," Jane whispered. "I want...to be...a sunbeam," she sighed.

"Jane, you *are* a sunbeam!" Cassandra consoled her, patting her hand. With that assurance, the patient relaxed and sank into another prolonged period of stillness.

"Her faith has always been so simple and so pure," remarked Henry.

"Yes—like that of a little child, replied Cassandra, looking at her lovingly.

That evening, as Cassandra took some rest, Henry sat by Jane's bed, his head in his hands, fighting back more powerful emotions than he had ever felt, except perhaps at his dear

Eliza's bedside as she lay dying of cancer. In fact, it almost felt like *deja vu* for him as he listened to his sister's erratic breathing. How difficult it was for him to say goodbye to this beloved sister! Slowly, a quietly inspired idea crept into his mind, and he began singing to her very softly,

> *Amazing grace! how sweet the sound*
> *That saved a wretch like me!*
> *I once was lost, but now am found;*
> *Was blind, but now I see.*

Jane's eyes blinked open, as she tried to focus on his beloved face.

> *'Twas grace that taught my heart to fear,*
> *And grace my fears relieved;*
> *How precious did that grace appear*
> *The hour I first believed!*

The dying patient's lips moved imperceptibly, but no sound came.

> *Through many dangers, toils and snares,*
> *I have already come;*
> *'Tis grace hath brought me safe thus far,*
> *And grace will lead me home.*

She stirred, eyes closed, as if the words were reaching deep into her soul, as Henry continued:

> *When we've been there ten thousand years,*
> *Bright, shining as the sun,*
> *We've no less days to sing God's praise*
> *Than when we'd first begun.*

Henry bent close to his sister's ear and whispered, "You're going to shine like the sun, Jane — just like our father. You're going to shine like Jesus."

The dying patient's lips moved once more, and Henry bent his head close, to hear — for the last time — "Oh, what a Henry!"

"Oh, what a Saviour!" he breathed, squeezing her hand gently.

Those were the last words they would ever exchange on this earth. As night closed in on them, Cassandra offered to take the next watch with her sister, for Henry had slept little the night before, and she had been able to rest during the day. They parted then — tears close to the surface in both. Cassandra sat close to the bed, cradling her sister in her arms as best she could. She dozed fitfully, waking with a start and trying to move to a more comfortable position. She thought of Tom Fowle, her *fiance*, who had died of Yellow Fever in the West Indies, and wondered if anyone had been comforting him as he departed this life. Midnight passed, and Cassandra counted the painful passing of the hours. She remembered her vigil with Jane at Henry's bedside as they prayed together for his recovery. She so wished that Jane would be spared and given more years to write. How could she ever survive without this dearest of sisters, with whom she was so close? There was no one in this world with whom she could share everything, like she did with Jane. But, around four-thirty that morning our celebrated authoress finally drew her last breath.

Cassandra, slowly taking in the reality, rose haltingly from her chair, bent over the inanimate body, and closed her sister's eyes. She stepped back and looked longingly at the lifeless form and was momentarily comforted to see a sweet serenity on her countenance. She went to the drawer for some scissors and lovingly snipped a lock of Jane's hair to keep as a memento. Then she awakened Henry, who rose immediately, and the two sat silently, hand in hand, awaiting the dawning of a new day.

As the city slowly began to stir, they could hear the schoolboys of Winchester College calling to one another on the streets below. They watched numbly at the window, wondering how everyone could be going about daily tasks oblivious to the momentous happenings in the little house with the bow window. Cassandra kept looking back at what appeared to her like a beautiful statue in the bed, shaking her head, unable to utter a sound. Henry finally was able to pull himself together long enough to send express messages to their family members, sharing with them the heartrending news. While he was out, he made arrangements for the simple wooden coffin in which she would be buried.

Edward and his son, William, were the first to come, from Chawton, looking grave and a little lost. Henry took William aside and gave him the sealed letter from his favourite Aunt. "It's the last thing she wrote, and you were very much on her mind and heart, William," he said kindly.

William looked at his Uncle, tears welling in his eyes. He took the precious paper, stared at it in amazement, and then tucked it in his waistcoat pocket. "I can't read it now, but I will...afterwards," he choked, as Henry gave him a warm, manly hug.

Later that day James Edward arrived from Steventon, as did Frank, thankfully still on home leave from the Navy. James, grief-stricken and indisposed, was not able to join them. And Charles, her particular little brother, was back at sea. The day of the funeral dawned damp and drizzling, matching precisely the mood of the mourners. Jane's three brothers and her nephew, James Edward, gently lifted the coffin containing the precious remains of their beloved relative. They bore it carefully down the stairs, with young William, head bowed and bravely choking back the tears, following closely behind them. The melancholy procession wended its way down the short street, disappearing too quickly around the corner toward the massive Cathedral.

Cassandra—denied by the custom of the day the opportunity to accompany her dear sister's body to its final resting place—leaned into the bow window, watching carefully until the little procession was completely out of sight. Alone and feeling that her heart had been wrenched out of her body, she stood for a long time as if spellbound, and then her whole being heaved with sobs of inconsolable grief. She sorrowed not as those who have no hope, but she knew that she would miss dreadfully this incomparable sister, who had been the soother of all of her sorrows. She knew not how long she remained there in the bow window.

After a time, when the first poignant pangs of her sorrow had passed, she was aware of a sudden warmth enveloping her. She opened her eyes slowly, squinting into a sunbeam of light streaming in on her through the window. When she was finally able to focus clearly, her gaze was carried upward to the tower of the Cathedral which was bathed in the same suffused light. In that moment her thoughts were drawn heavenward, where her sweet sister seemed to be smiling down on her. "Jane!" she breathed "you were the sun of my life, the gilder of my every pleasure."

Cassandra stood there a little longer, transfixed—trying to take in the significance of this memorable moment that would remain with her for the rest of her life. In that instant she suddenly realized that her loss was heaven's gain, and she was reminded anew that she would one day be reunited with her beloved sister in that blessed abode. Finally, feeling profoundly comforted and strengthened, she sighed softly into the sunlight, "How much we all will miss her!"

Chapter 12

A Letter to William Knight

8 College Street, Winchester

My dearest William,

Words fail me when I want to express to you how much I love and admire you, my dear nephew. We have always been very close from the beginning of your life, for I was at Godmersham when you were born—can it be nineteen years ago?—and you have been special to me ever since!

If I should try to explain why you are so appealing to me, I would want to tell you that everything about you is so natural—your affections, your manners, and your drollery. How alike we are with regard to that latter characteristic, William! And I must confess that you entertain and interest me extremely with your winsome ways. I assure you that even though you bear the name Knight, and not Austen, you will always be my Knight in shining armour!

After you were with us recently for two pleasant months at Chawton cottage, I remember writing to your sister, Fanny, and relating to her that you and I are the very best of friends. I recall telling her that I love you very much indeed. But then I had to add that so do we all, for you are quite our own William, with your excellent looks and fine appetite. You always seem so perfectly well, William—the picture of health in spirit, soul, and body. We are similar in the first two aspects, you and I, but I fear my body has not been keeping up with my soul and spirit lately!

I have enjoyed our long discussions about the characters in my novels—especially the clergymen. I am so glad that you like them all, and the way I have tried to differentiate among them and give them peculiarities all their own. I recall that you particularly liked Edward Ferrars, of *Sense and Sensibility*, despite his naughty secret engagement. But you considered Edmund Bertram, in *Mansfield Park*, not far behind him in worth, once he had the sense to fall in love with Fanny! How we laughed together at Mr. Collins, of *Pride and Prejudice,* and Mr. Elton, in *Emma*, who were both out of their wits most of the time.

But we agreed they all have their charms—like you, dear William! Are they not true sketches of clergymen with whom you have been acquainted? And you may soon discover the delightful Henry Tilney in another novel that I have in hand at the moment. With your strong sense of the ridiculous, I am sure that you will appreciate this clergyman. So now you have all these examples of clergymen from the pen of your Aunt Jane to either imitate or avoid!

Seriously, William, I want to wish you godspeed in your plans to take Holy Orders and become the next Rector of Steventon Church. Your papa, and especially your dear, departed grandpapa, will be so proud that you are carrying on the care of that flock. And your Uncle James and Uncle Henry will undoubtedly be of great assistance to you in your aspirations. Perhaps Uncle Henry will even help you in the publishing of some of the fine sermons you will preach at Steventon!

I know that your affections and your manners will eminently suit you for this responsibility. Indeed, your congregation will love you dearly, as I do! And if I am not in this world long enough to see you ordained, be assured, dearest nephew, that I will be a part of that great cloud of witnesses that will be watching you from above! So, do not think of me lying in a tomb in Winchester Cathedral. But when you see a cloud floating on high, with perhaps a ray of sun shining from behind it, consider that it is your Aunt Jane encouraging you as you use your considerable gifts to further God's great kingdom!

Your always affectionate and loving aunt,
Jane Austen

Inscription on Jane Austen's Grave in
Winchester Cathedral

In Memory of
JANE AUSTEN
youngest daughter of the late
Revd GEORGE AUSTEN,
formerly Rector of Steventon in this County.
She departed this Life on the 18th of July 1817,
aged 41, after a long illness supported with
the patience and the hopes of a Christian.

The benevolence of her heart,
the sweetness of her temper, and
the extraordinary endowments of her mind
obtained the regard of all who knew her and
the warmest love of her intimate connections.

Their grief is in proportion to their affection,
they know their loss to be irreparable,
but in their deepest affliction they are consoled
by a firm though humble hope that her charity,
devotion, faith, and purity have rendered
her soul acceptable in the sight of her
REDEEMER.

Printed in the United States
201866BV00001B/217-1224/P